Nightmares

BY PETER NEALEN

This is a work of fiction. Characters, locations, and incidents are products of the author's imagination.

Printed in the United States of America

http://americanpraetorians.wordpress.com

http://www.facebook.com/PeteNealenAuthor

Chapter 1

Security was set and the sun was going down over the Jordanian border. We had the Humvees in a circle, turrets facing outboard, in the bottom of a wide wadi. Most of the other Marines, who weren't up on the guns, were already stretching out on the ground or the hoods and roofs of the trucks.

I joined the other Assistant Team Leaders and Gunny at the command truck, in the middle of the circle. There wasn't much to go over; the op was going as according to plan as it was ever going to. That meant we hadn't found any sign of the smuggling route that was supposed to be moving insurgents and munitions into Iraq from Syria. I'd pointed out during mission planning that up north along the Euphrates was more likely than out here in the middle of the empty desert, and while Gunny had agreed, there wasn't much any of us could do about it. This was the mission, so we were going to do it as best we could. Comb the desert, aye, aye, sir.

We talked about some inconsequential BS for a while, peppered with cynical jokes and wisecracks that would have gravely offended anyone not familiar with the kind of twisted sense of humor you develop in combat arms, before drifting off to our trucks to get some shut-eye until it was our turn to take security. Nobody expected anyone to be out here in the daytime, much less at night. Hajji slept at night; none of us had ever seen any sort of night operations run by the insurgents, and finding an Iraqi farmer out after dark was next to completely unknown. Not

1

that we'd seen any farms out here; the most habitation we'd seen in five days was a single Bedouin tent three days before.

I pulled my iso-mat out of my ruck, which was hanging by a snap-link on the side of our truck, and unrolled it on the ground beside the rear tire. It was still way too hot to use a poncho liner, especially since I wasn't going to take off my cammies or boots. Empty desert or not, bad habits were bad habits, and we weren't going to stop being careful just because we hadn't seen a soul besides each other for three days.

It was hot enough that I couldn't go to sleep immediately, but just lay there, letting my mind wander.

After a while, I suddenly noticed that my thoughts had wandered into some seriously dark territory. A formless disquiet had settled on my mind, coupled with a sense of being watched. It was a feeling I'd experienced before, when I'd been sure there were bad guys close. I just called it the heebie-jeebies most of the time, but I always followed up on it, just in case. I sat up, grabbing my rifle from where it was leaning against the truck.

My first instinct was to check the perimeter. With the sun gone, the desert was nothing but empty darkness. The stars had come out, but the moon was still below the horizon. It wouldn't be up for hours.

Something made me turn around. There was a figure standing in the middle of the laager site. Any thoughts that one of the other Marines was walking around died instantly. This thing was taller than any of us, appeared to be wearing a cloak or thobe, and was blacker than any of the surrounding darkness.

Except for its eyes. Those were points of bright flame.

It stared directly at me for a second, while I was frozen in place, unable to process what I was looking at. Then its mouth gaped in a glowing, sulfurous grin, its teeth jagged black fangs against the furnace burning inside. Still looking back at me, it turned and brought a long arm slashing downward and smashed the command Humvee in half.

With a violent sweep of both incredibly long arms, it threw the two halves in opposite directions, sending them spinning through the air to impact with crushing force against two more trucks, reducing them to twisted metal and killing the men sleeping in and around them.

2

Gunny hadn't been sleeping at the command truck; he'd been over near my vehicle. He was already up and moving, trying to get an angle on the thing. The sight reminded me of the rifle in my own hands, and I brought it to my shoulder, flicking the selector off safe and trying to pick up the thing in my ACOG in the dark.

It was too fast. In the time it took to blink, it was on the other side of the laager site, sweeping two more Marines off the ground by their throats. They burst into screaming flames in its hands, and it threw them out into the desert, shrieking out their last breaths as they burned.

Gunny opened fire at that point. I joined in a moment later, as my brain finally got out of the screaming lock it had been in since that thing had grinned at me. We might hit the Marines in that truck, but if we didn't kill that thing, or at least drive it off, we were all going to die.

"Mac!" I bellowed over the hammering of our rifle fire, "Get that gun up and shoot that thing!"

Mackenzie, my gunner, had already started swinging the turret around and opened up with the .50, the hammering thunder almost driving me to my knees as it blasted just over my head.

The heavy rounds flashed and sparked, and the thing disappeared in a cloud of dust and smoke as the .50 was joined by the 240 on Gunny's truck, hammering at the thing and the Humvee behind it. The men in that truck were dead, if not by the creature's hands, then by our fire. But we had no choice. It was shoot or die, and none of us wanted to die in that godforsaken desert, at least not without a fight.

Finally, Gunny yelled, "Cease fire! Cease fire!" It took a couple of minutes and both of the surviving heavy guns going dry before anybody stopped shooting. I hastily shrugged into my vest and reloaded as I joined Gunny to carefully advance on the blasted wreckage where we'd last seen the thing.

There was no sign of it. Just smashed, burned bodies and a Humvee reduced to twisted wreckage.

I awoke with a start, the image of fiery eyes in a smoky, featureless face still seeming to float in my vision even after I was awake. I looked desperately around the room, disoriented as hell, until I remembered where I was; a small, cheap, ratty motel room in Bend, Oregon.

With a groan, I sat up on the rickety, and now sweat-soaked, bed. It creaked and swayed alarmingly under me, or at least it would have been alarming if the rest of the room hadn't been swaying along with it. My head was already starting to pound, and my mouth tasted like a small animal had died in it.

I reached for the bottle of Jack on the nightstand to try to wash both the taste and the vision out, but in my drunken fumbling, I knocked it off and onto the floor. I scrambled to grab it before too much spilled out, but when I picked it up and brought it to my lips, it was empty. I threw it across the room in frustration.

Every night. Every blasted night since that night in western Al Anbar, the same nightmare kept coming back, mingling with an ever-present sense of unease and fear until there wasn't a lot of difference between the nightmares and the waking world. That night had changed my life; I'd been in hell ever since.

I heaved myself to my feet. It took a couple of tries, and when I finally got upright, the room was spinning and I swayed dangerously. But eventually I was able to stagger over to the small table in the corner, in search of the second bottle of Jack Daniels I'd bought that afternoon.

That was when I discovered that the empty I'd tossed *was* the second bottle. I swore, the word sounding slurred even in my ears. Well, that wouldn't do. There was no way I was going back to Nightmare-Land without more booze.

It took way too long to struggle into my jeans, well-worn Marine combat boots, and jacket. I almost forgot the key on the way out, but since it was an old fashioned metal one instead of one of the newer keycards, I couldn't have locked it in the room anyway, so it probably didn't matter that much. It wasn't like I had much of anything in the room to get stolen.

Even as drunk as I was, I still had enough of a shred of judgment left that I knew I shouldn't drive. I started my slow, weaving way down the street, looking for a liquor store that might still be open. I didn't even know what time it was; I hadn't bothered to check, and my watch was somewhere in the room. I didn't care. The only thing that mattered was trying to drink the

4

dreams away. It hadn't worked yet, but it had to eventually. That's what I kept telling myself, anyway.

I don't know how long I wandered the streets. There was hardly any traffic at all. It still took me a while to realize there was a car pacing me.

It wasn't new, but it wasn't a junker gang-banger car, either. Not that I was in any shape to do anything about some gang punks getting their jollies by beating up a drunk in the middle of the night...

The passenger side window was rolled down. A silver-haired oldster dressed in black was driving. "You all right, son?" he asked.

I was focusing on him instead of where I was going, and stepped off the curb by accident. I just about face-planted into his fender. "Fine," I slurred.

"You sure don't look it," he replied. "Come on, get in, I'll give you a lift."

I realized I was in no shape to refuse, so I struggled with the door and slumped into the passenger seat. It took a couple of tries to get the door shut. Then I just sat there for a moment, my head back against the headrest. I was beyond caring who the old guy was, or what his motive for picking up a drunk on the side of the street was.

He slowly pulled the car away from the curb. I kept my eyes closed; it lessened the disorientation.

"Where are you trying to go?" he asked after a few moments.

"Somewhere with booze," I replied.

"No offense, son, but you don't look like you need any more booze," he said sternly. I cracked an eye at him. He was half watching the road, half watching me, and there was no timidity on that craggy slab of a face. Through my haze, I could somehow tell that this was no well-meaning but naïve old man. That wasn't the voice of a clueless do-gooder.

So, in spite of how pissed-off and miserable I was, instead of harsh words about minding his own business, I just leaned back on the headrest and said, "I still haven't had enough to make the nightmares stop."

There was a different tone to his voice when he replied, "That much booze doesn't exist on the face of the Earth, my friend." There was a pause, while the night went by outside the car. "Where are you staying?"

"I take it that means you're not going to drop me off at a liquor store?"

He chuckled. "Nope. Even if I was inclined to aid and abet your self-destruction, there aren't any open at this time of night. So, where are you staying?"

"The Dall Motel," I replied.

"That pesthole?" He sounded incensed. "Tell you what, we'll go there, pick up your things, and you can crash on my couch for the night."

"Why?" I asked.

He stared at the road for a moment. "I've seen a lot of suffering in my day, son," he replied. "Experienced a fair bit of it, too. If I can alleviate even a little bit of it, well, I believe that's worthwhile."

"I don't need a Good Samaritan, old man," I said, closing my eyes again.

He gave another dry chuckle. "'Good Samaritan' is pretty close to my job description, son. We're here."

I opened my eyes, and sure enough, we were sitting in the neon-lit parking lot. Somehow the dump of a motel looked even worse in the purple and red light. I fumbled with the door handle, got the door open, levered myself out, and promptly fell on my hands and knees and vomited on the asphalt.

Surprisingly strong hands gripped me under the armpits and lifted me off the ground and back into the car. "Give me the key," he said. "I'll get your stuff, and then we'll go."

"My truck..." I started to say.

"We'll come back and get it when you're sober," he said. He held out a hand for the room key. I had to search my pockets to remember where I'd shoved it. When I handed it to him, I noticed he was wearing a Roman collar for the first time.

"You're a priest," I mumbled stupidly.

He smiled faintly. "Yes, I am. Now just sit there; I'll be back in a minute."

I might have passed out for a little bit there; it seemed like an eyeblink later he was back at the car, with my pathetic pack full of what little I had with me. "Is this all, son?" he asked.

I just nodded. I didn't have much anymore. Some of my stuff I'd sold, some I'd just lost track of in my drunken haze over the last few months since I separated from the Marine Corps. He put the pack in the back seat, then got behind the wheel again.

I don't remember much of the drive to the rectory. I vaguely remember him pulling me out of the passenger seat and slinging my arm around his shoulders as he helped me into the house and lowered me onto the couch in the living room. After that, it all just goes a little black.

For the first time in months, the dreams left me alone. I woke up to the sun streaming through the front windows, feeling better than I had in what felt like ages. I still didn't feel good, mind you, but better than rock bottom is still better. I was still in my clothes, though my boots were off and on the floor at the end of the couch.

The rectory was quiet. There was an old grandfather clock in the corner of the living room that ticked quietly, keeping the silence from being absolute. After a few moments of gathering myself together, I started to hear some rustling and low speech from the back rooms, so I padded over to investigate. My head was splitting, but I was somewhat clearer.

Past the tiny kitchen, I found a small study, practically overflowing with books, with an ancient, well-worn writing desk and three chairs. The Father was sitting at the desk, and another man was sitting in one of the armchairs.

The other guy turned to look at me as I walked in. He looked like he was in his mid-forties, but his eyes looked like he'd seen far more than forty years. His hair, cropped short, was going gray at the temples, and his face was weathered and clean-shaven. He was dressed in jeans and a t-shirt under a leather jacket, and the way he was sitting, he could easily get at the big Magnum revolver on his hip and train it on the door.

Father O'Neal turned from his desk, wheeling the chair away. "How are you feeling?" he asked. The man in the armchair didn't say anything, but just studied me with an intensity I found increasingly uncomfortable even through the haze of my hangover.

"Like I got hit by a truck," I replied. "But I guess I'm alive."

"Breakfast?" he asked. My stomach did a flip-flop at the idea, and I imagine I turned a little green.

"I don't think I could eat much right now," I admitted.

He shook his head. "Food's the only way you're going to kill that hangover, son," he said. "There's some bread and butter in the kitchen to get you started."

After some hesitation as my head throbbed, I nodded and headed into the little kitchen. After a few bites, I actually started to feel a little more human. I wandered back into the book-lined study, chewing as I went, and sank into the other armchair.

The other guy was still studying me with that intense, unnerving stare. His eyes were dark gray, almost blue but not quite. I'm not usually one for studying another dude's eyes, but when they're boring into you like they could set you on fire by just staring at you, they tend to get your attention.

As my head cleared, I started to sense the tension in the room rising. Neither man said anything, but just watched me eat. Finally, I finished chewing, swallowed, and said, "Mister, just what are you staring at?"

His expression didn't change, but he leaned back in the chair a bit. "So, you're Jed Horn."

That cut through my hangover more than the food or the tense silence of the room had. "How do you know that?" I asked, the last of the bread forgotten.

"I've been looking for you," he replied. He reached down beside the chair, and I tensed. It wasn't an entirely rational reaction; he obviously wasn't reaching for his Magnum and I wasn't in any shape to do anything if he was planning to attack me anyway. He came up with a manila folder and tossed it casually in my lap.

I stared at him for a moment before reaching down to open the folder. When I saw the pictures inside, I almost retched.

They were crime scene photos. At least, they were labeled that way. And they were gruesome.

The first was of a young man hanging by the neck from the rafters of what looked like an abandoned building somewhere. Maybe a barn. The surroundings were kind of lost in the fact that he was a hanged corpse, and that his eyes had apparently been gouged out. Blood and destroyed tissue had flowed down his face.

8

The others were worse. Two more young men and a young woman were lying on the floor around the hanged man. All had had their eyes gouged out, and then had been eviscerated. Their intestines had been wrapped around their wrists and throats. It was worse than anything I'd ever seen in Iraq, even the night the...*thing* came calling.

I looked up at the two of them, sickened. Both were still watching me coolly. "Recognize them?" the guy with the Magnum asked.

I looked down at the pictures again, trying to study the disfigured faces without losing what little was left in my stomach. It took a couple minutes of just staring, trying to see past the horror, before it struck me.

"John Samuels," I whispered. Samuels had been the founder of Idaho State Paranormal, a small ghost hunter/paranormal investigation group. I was pretty sure at least one of the mutilated bodies at his feet had been Jenny Carter, his girlfriend and the group's primary records keeper. The other two had to be Matt and Fred.

I'd spent a month investigating two haunted houses with those people. I'd last seen them only a week and a half before.

The graying man handed me another folder. More crime scene photos. More horrifying mutilations. Only two people this time, but similarly killed, with one hanging by the neck. I couldn't recognize them, the disfiguring injuries were so bad, but the notes said they were Adam Kosh and Vince Kennard. They were both occult historians I'd gotten to know in Boise.

I looked up at those cold gray eyes. "You think I did this?" I asked hoarsely. I could hear my own heartbeat and I felt a little faint.

He shook his head. 'No, I don't. Neither do the cops, in case you were worried on that count. There's no forensic evidence to suggest there was ever anyone else in the rooms where these murders were committed. In fact, they've both been classed as 'murder-suicide,' with the hanged man in each case being deemed the murderer."

He leaned forward in his chair. "I've been looking for you because you spent a great deal of time with both of these groups until about a week before they died.

9

"Why are you spending so much time with ghost hunters and occultists, Jed?"

I stared at him. Instead of answering him, I asked a question of my own. "Are you FBI or something? How did you know I was here?"

He inclined his head toward the priest. "Father O'Neal called me and told me he'd found you. I've had people from Yuba City to Walla Walla looking for you. And no, I'm not a Fed."

Father O'Neal spoke for the first time since I'd come back into the study. "Jed, the question is serious. Why have you spent so much time looking into this occult stuff?"

I looked at him, then back at the guy with the Magnum. Why did they want to know? If he wasn't a Fed, then why was he looking for me? I was suddenly all too aware of the fact my Colt was in my backpack and nowhere near me, while old boy with the scary eyes was a gesture away from that big hand cannon.

Father O'Neal seemed to sense what was going on in my head. "Dan, why don't you let me handle this for a minute?" he asked. When Dan's eyebrow went up, he just said, "Trust me."

Dan studied me for a moment, then got up and left the room without another word. Father O'Neal leaned back in his chair, stared at the crucifix over the door for a moment, then looked at me.

"Jed, what I'm going to say next is going to sound like either the weirdest thing you've ever heard, or the ramblings of some frightened evangelical housewife who just found out her teenage precious is playing Dungeons and Dragons. But if you've been looking into this stuff as intently as Dan says you have, then you've probably got some idea of what's going on.

"But first I've got to know; why *have* you been looking into this stuff, Jed? You don't act like some curious kid who's watched too many ghost reality shows."

I frowned, studying his face. So far, the number of people I'd talked to about what had happened out in the desert was vanishingly small. None of the paranormal investigators—who were now corpses—had known why I was joining them. I thought that even they would think I was crazy. That's what the Navy shrinks had said. They'd said we had all hallucinated the thing with the burning eyes.

But for some reason, that to this day I can't quite articulate, I told Father O'Neal. I told him the whole story, starting with the attack, then the Marine Corps' reaction to what we said had happened, then the search for answers after we got out. I told him about the spiritualists, mediums, occultists, and paranormal investigators I'd met with over the last year. I told him about how I didn't even think about making a living anymore; I was obsessed with proving, if only to myself, that I wasn't crazy.

I told him about the nightmares and how they kept getting worse; how I tried to drink them away until life was a haze of alcohol and fear.

Somehow in the outpouring of words I kind of lost track of the here-and-now fears of why a man with a massive revolver was looking for me, and asking questions about people I'd made friends with, who were now dead.

"You're not crazy." Apparently Dan had only left the room far enough to make it feel like he wasn't listening. "What hit you guys out in the desert was an ifrit. Fire djinn. I've heard of them, but never seen one; they tend to stay on that side of the pond." He sat back down in the armchair. Father O'Neal frowned at him. He shrugged apologetically. "Sorry, Father. I don't think we've really got time to be polite about this." He turned to me. "The fact is, kid, you've been playing with fire.

"The occult is real. *Very* real, and *very* dangerous. There are things lurking in the shadows of this world that could kill you with a thought. The only reason they haven't devoured the human race as a whole is that they're not *allowed* to."

"Allowed by what?" I asked.

"Who do you think?" Father O'Neal said.

"There's a war going on," Dan went on, "and it has been going on since the beginning of time. God and His angels on one side, the demons and some of their cronies in the Otherworld on the other. There are rules of engagement, but within those rules, it's the deadliest war you've ever even imagined. And those who are poking around without knowing those rules are essentially wandering blind into a minefield.

"You want to know why I was looking for you? I've seen lots of kids get into the occult over the years, lost and drifting. Some have been able to get clear; others haven't. Some have died because of it, like those poor souls." He pointed to the pictures on my lap. "Sometimes, they become focal points for something worse."

"You mean I'm a…what? A carrier, or something?" I asked. I gripped the arms of the chair. It felt like the floor was opening up beneath me. It was bad enough when I thought that I was just trying to prove I wasn't crazy. Now I was finding out some of the depth of the horror that I'd stumbled into, and it was making my head spin a little. I tasted bile in the back of my mouth.

"We think something's following you," Father O'Neal said. "We don't know what, but it's murdered at least two groups that you've had dealings with, in similar ways. This happens sometimes, especially with those who start inquiring into the occult without the spiritual foundation to help keep the dark things at bay."

"You've attracted closer attention that most people ever do," Dan said. "So now you've got a choice. You can tell us to get lost, and continue on the way you've been going. It's more than likely that if you do that, even if I can hunt down and banish whatever it is that's following you, you'll end up either like them"—he gestured again to the photos—"or attracting something worse. Worst case; you go all the way over, start willingly trafficking with demons, and somebody like me has to put you down, hopefully before you drag anyone else down with you."

I gathered myself enough to scoff a little. While most of this was kind of a shock, I guess I'd gotten inured enough over the last year or so that I was able to mentally adjust pretty easily, hangover or no hangover, to the idea that I was sitting in a priest's study discussing demons and monsters like it was a sane and rational thing to discuss. I'd seen what I'd seen in the desert, and seen some weird stuff since, but I still wasn't entirely used to thinking of this stuff as anything but crazy.

"Why would I start dealing with demons, if that's what these things are?" I demanded. "One of them killed half my platoon."

"Ifrits aren't demons," Dan snapped. "They're something else. Demons are subtle. They get in your head. They have you trapped before you even know it. Something will offer you a

12

solution, if you just bend a *little*. Then a little more. Then you're damned before you even realize it, and by the time you do realize it, you don't care anymore. As soon as you start thinking you're too smart for them, they've got you. Arrogance will destroy you in this world." He straightened a little bit in his chair. "Ultimatum time, kid. You're pretty much down to two options. You can't go back; you've noticed the things that go bump in the night, and they know it. You'll never be able to live without something watching you, or looking over your shoulder for what might be lurking in the dark. Like I said, you can keep blundering around until you get more people hurt and probably lose your own soul in the process, or you can come with me.

"This is my living, my calling. I hunt these things. Father O'Neal's one of the few who knows about us; most of the world would rather not think we're anything but kooks. They don't want to accept that there are things more powerful than Man, things that can still threaten us in the dark.

"It'll mean sacrifice. It's not easy. I can't say you'll ever sleep soundly again; but then, it doesn't sound like you're getting much beauty sleep right now anyway. But you'll have a better chance of ending up on the right side of things when all is said and done."

"What'll it be, Jed?" Father O'Neal asked quietly.

It didn't take all that long to decide. I knew that there was *something* out there; the ones called it superstition or delusion hadn't seen what I had. These two didn't seem to be nuts to me, and they accepted that what had happened to us had indeed happened. And there were those murders to consider. If something or someone was indeed following me to commit such atrocities, I wanted to deal with it.

And, on a more visceral level, I knew I was on a downward slide. It wasn't just the nightmares, the booze, and the haunted hangovers. My grip on sanity, regardless of whether or not I'd really seen what I'd seen, was slipping, and, deep down, I knew it. I hadn't been able to lift my eyes to anything good in a long time. Waking or sleeping, I was haunted by disquiet and a sense of ever-present doom that never went away. I felt lost in a wilderness of horror, and I knew there was only one other way out if I didn't take Father and Dan up on their offer.

13

Father O'Neal heard my first Confession in almost two years. It felt like a great weight had been lifted off my shoulders. After that, preparations were pretty brief. I didn't have much. Father O'Neal assured me he'd take care of my truck. If both Dan and I rode in his Bronco, not only would it save on gas, but he could instruct me as we drove. We rolled out of town and toward Idaho, and the dead friends I'd inadvertently betrayed.

Chapter 2

The old, abandoned motel where John Samuels and his friends had died was just outside of town. The parking lot was webbed with weed-filled cracks, the windows were all broken where they weren't boarded up, and the bushes and trees around the lot had overgrown to the point that the branches were brushing the roof. The grounds were covered in weeds, fallen leaves, and pine needles. The falling-down, broken sign in the parking lot had once said, "The Drop Inn."

While a small strip mall with a McDonalds and two gas stations was less than a quarter mile away, no one seemed to be coming close to the old motel if they could avoid it. There weren't any vehicles parked nearby, and all of the police line tape had been taken down. A couple of bits of the yellow plastic were still tied to a couple of the trees, where it had apparently just been torn off instead of untied.

"I would have thought a crime scene would still be blocked off," I commented, as we got out of the Bronco, watching the motel.

"Not if it's cut and dried," he said. "It does seem a *little* early, but since they declared it a murder-suicide at least a week ago, there probably isn't much more they can get from it evidence-wise. At least that's my thought."

I followed as he started to walk toward the front door. I kept looking around. "It just seems to me that there'd be more scrutiny if something was weird and, well, off. Like 'men in black suits with Ray-Bans that never come off' or something."

Dan snorted. "The official position of ninety-nine percent of politicians is that there's no God, and certainly no Devil. It makes it easier for 'em. It removes the possibility of eternal consequences for the crap they pull. So, some sort of 'Bureau of Paranormal Research and Defense' or some such wouldn't make it past the first aide's desk. That would require acknowledging something that nobody in the halls of politics and bureaucracy wants to acknowledge."

"I've seen plenty of hypocrisy and cognitive dissonance from politicians before," I pointed out.

"Sure," he said, stepping up to the door to the lobby. The glass had been shattered a long time ago, and fragments crunched underfoot. More police line tape hung from the doorframe. "Trust me, though. This world is something that no amount of legislation or tax money can even scratch. That scares 'em enough that they won't even consider it exists." He swung the door open; it was still hanging from its hinges, though there was no glass in it. "I'm sure there are some really frustrated detectives out here right now, who are being told by their bosses that the case is closed and that they have to concentrate on other things now." He looked over his shoulder, past me, into the parking lot. "So keep an eye out; I wouldn't be surprised if one or more of them comes back, poking around here for clues after hours."

"You don't expect them to find any?" I asked, as I followed him into the lobby. There was no furniture left aside from the front desk. Bare wires hung from the ceiling where the lights had been, and some of the tile on the floor was broken, fragments scattered in the corners. The place was a wreck.

He shook his head. "They don't know what to look for." He was scanning the walls and ceiling.

I followed his gaze, but didn't see anything but stained, peeling wallpaper and crumbling ceiling tiles. "I'm afraid I don't, either," I said.

He chuckled. "Well, that's why you're here with me. To learn. Come on." He led the way out of the lobby and down the hallway between the rooms.

"Would ghosts leave some kind of evidence?" I asked.

He shook his head as he led the way toward the room where John had died. "Ghosts don't actually do anything. They have no impact on the physical world. Human beings have bodies to do that, and the dead don't have bodies. The fact that they can occasionally be seen or heard by those who have some sensitivity to spirits doesn't lessen that fact."

"So hauntings aren't real?" I asked.

He led the way into the room. "They can be. Sometimes they're nothing more than settling houses or hallucinations; once I checked one out that turned out to be a methane leak bad enough it was causing the family to go hypoxic while the doors and windows were shut.

"Other times, there genuinely is something screwing with the family, or anyone who comes to the 'haunted' place. Most of the really hostile ones are demonic; some of the more violent hauntings, with some sort of really bad crime behind them, aren't because of unquiet ghosts, but because the evil committed invited a demon in. Most of the time, though, the mischievous or simply annoying types are some sort of Otherworlders."

"You've mentioned 'Otherworlders' before," I said, as we looked around at the bare walls. The room didn't look all that different from the lobby, except for the ratty, stained carpet underfoot instead of tile. There was a huge, dark stain in the center of the room, and the ceiling tiles had been stripped, one of the structural members slightly bent from the weight of John's corpse. "I'm not sure I get what you're talking about."

He was moving around the room, carefully examining every inch of the wall. "Demons are pure spirit; while they have the power to affect the physical world, they are not of it. Most of them are caged in what we variously call Hell or the Abyss. Most in this line of work call it the Abyss; *Hell* comes too close to invocation. The more you talk about some of these things, especially the really bad ones, the more attention you invite. And let me assure you, you *don't* want to attract that kind of attention if you can help it."

He started peeling back some of the wallpaper in the corner of the room. "The Otherworld is what used to be called 'Faerie,' or 'The Other Side.' It's not so much a place as it is a category; creatures that are somewhere between people and spirits. Father O'Neal used to like to describe it as 'the world that's just out of sight.'"

"Father O'Neal knows a lot about all of this?" I asked, looking over his shoulder as he dug at the wallpaper.

He chuckled. "Ben O'Neal was a legend. Probably the greatest Witch Hunter in the world until he quit the Order to become a priest. He ran into a Poj Nxtoog near Quang Tri in '69. He dealt with it, drove on, got out, and found the Order. He joined up as soon as he found out the Order existed, and never looked back. He walked through some of the darkest places on Earth for twenty years, then quit to go to the seminary. If you've ever got a question, Father O'Neal will have the answer. If he won't tell you, stop asking."

He tore a big chunk of wallpaper off, but before I could get a good look at what he was looking at underneath, every door in the motel that was still on its hinges slammed shut at the same time.

I jumped, but Dan didn't seem ruffled at all. He just looked up at the door. "Well, that's not good," he said mildly.

The whole motel creaked and groaned like a house in a storm, but there was no wind. I faced the door, my old Colt 1911 in my hand, but I wasn't sure what I was going to do with it. Images of the ifrit (it seemed a little strange, having a name for that thing) flitted through my mind, along with the old fear. We'd shot the hell out of that thing, and hadn't scratched it. What was I going to do with a pistol against another one?

The door suddenly opened about a foot, then slammed shut again. There was a noise that I couldn't identify out in the hall; it sounded almost like a snarl, but after I heard it I couldn't be sure I'd actually heard anything at all. Then I unmistakably heard what sounded like light, fast footsteps.

Suddenly there was a tiny pair of hands grabbing my jeans just below my knees. I jerked and looked down, pointing my Colt at whatever had grabbed me.

Dan seized my wrist and shook his head before I could shoot. I squinted down at the tiny figure.

It was hard to see all that well in the gloom of the abandoned room. I got an impression of a crooked body with overly long, wiry arms, a big head, pointed nose, and beady eyes that seemed to glint even in the dimness.

"You're Hunters, aren't you?" The voice was thin and squeaky, with a bit of an odd accent. "You've got to help me! I never hurt anybody! Just a bit of fun, scaring teenagers! I didn't do anything, but now he wants to eat me!"

Dan had an intricately worked silver crucifix out of his shirt, hanging on a silver chain, and that cannon of a revolver in his right hand. Father O'Neal had given me a similar crucifix, so I pulled it out like Dan had. It seemed like the thing to do. "You were the 'haunting?'" he asked.

The bulbous head nodded. "Yeah, yeah. It was just fun, no harm done. Make some noises, move some stuff when nobody's looking, toss a few things. Scare the daylights out of some teenagers. Watch them run and scream; it was hilarious. Nothing bad. Nothing evil.

"Then *it* came. It was bad, wrong, scary. I ran and hid. They were stupid. They never saw it coming. It cursed them, then tore them apart. Then, after it was gone, this other one came, and now he's after me! You've got to do something!"

"You're going to have to tell us more than that," Dan said. "What was 'it,' and what is 'he?'"

"I don't know what it was," the little figure said. "I only know it smelled *wrong*. There was a whiff of smoke and fire around it, behind a sort of sour smell. It wasn't one of us. I could feel its hate. So I hid. It didn't look for me; it just waited for them, and it killed them."

The little guy seemed to shrink back as the door rattled like somebody was trying to open it. It wasn't locked; the latch wasn't even still in the door. There was just a hole where the knob had been. But something was apparently keeping it closed. "You know what *he* is. They're always drawn to places like this."

Dan was watching the door, his eyes narrowed. I was looking between the door, Dan, and the little gray…person clinging to my pants leg. The figure was carefully keeping my leg between him and the door. "Uh," I managed, "what's…he… talking about?" I asked Dan.

The little gray guy looked up at me, and squinted. "Oh, man," he squeaked. "A new guy!"

"Shut up," Dan told him. He didn't take his eyes off the door, which was really starting to bang and rattle in the doorframe. I still had no idea what was keeping it closed. "Remember I said that ghosts can't actually do anything to affect the physical world? Well, poltergeists are either Otherworld pranksters like this little toad..."

"Hey!" the little guy protested, even as he shrank back even more behind me when the loudest bang yet came from the door.

"...or they're demonic. Certain acts of violence open doors to these things just as surely as deliberate witchcraft. Lesser class of demon, but *any* demon is dangerous. They're like flies to a corpse." He lifted that big revolver and aimed it at the door. Latin rolled off his tongue, almost, but not quite, drowned out by the thunder of the revolver as he fired three shots through the door. I clapped my hands over my ears, knocking myself in the side of the head with my own pistol in the process, just in time to keep from being completely deafened by the reports.

The door stopped rattling. For a moment, there was silence.

Dan still had that hand cannon pointed at the door. Everything seemed still, waiting, but I got the distinct feeling that it was only a calm before a storm.

Dan broke the silence. "Jed, have you got a flashlight?"

I kicked myself. I should have thought of that, going into a darkened, abandoned building, but I hadn't, since it was daytime outside. I was getting rusty. "No," I admitted.

Without taking his eyes or his gun muzzle off the door, he reached into a pocket and pulled out a small, aluminum flashlight. He held it out, and I stepped over to take it, only then realizing that the little...person was still trying to hide behind my leg. I shook him off, to his squeal of dismay, and took the light.

"Take a look at that symbol on the wall over there and tell me if you recognize it," Dan said. He was still covering the door. So far, there hadn't been any new noises.

I had to try not to tread on the little gray guy, as he was still trying to shelter around my legs like a scared puppy. It was tempting to kick him out of the way, but something told me I

20

probably shouldn't. Dan hadn't been particularly friendly toward the little creature, but he hadn't been unnecessarily harsh, either. I realized I was entirely ignorant of the rules here. I had a lot to learn, no matter how much I'd been poking around the darker side of existence for the last year.

I shined the light on the wall. There was a symbol scrawled on the drywall behind the wallpaper. It looked disturbing, even as abstract as it was. It also looked kind of familiar.

"Yeah, I think I have seen this before," I said. "It was in a book..." I wracked my brain to try to remember where. I snapped my fingers. "There was a professor... What was his name? Ashton, that was it. Clark Ashton; he taught at a little college in Colorado. Howard Phillips College. Little liberal-arts college. Ashton actually teaches Occult Studies. I talked to him for a while."

"Hmm. Sounds like he took more of an interest in you than you might have thought," Dan mused. He was still watching the door. There hadn't been any more noises or movement. "I guess we're heading for Colorado, then."

I looked toward the door. "Is it gone?" I asked.

He shook his head. "I doubt it. It's waiting." He stepped toward the door. "Come on. Waiting on it isn't going to help any."

I flexed my hand around the grip of my pistol. Suddenly the little guy was grabbing my pantleg again. I gritted my teeth as I resisted the urge to punt him into the wall.

"Wait!" he screeched. "What about me?! You can't leave me here to get eaten!"

Dan took his eyes off the door just long enough to shoot the little guy a hard look as he flipped the revolver's cylinder open, pried out the empties, and thumbed three fresh cartridges in. "We won't be leaving it here if we can help it," he said, "but don't think we're going to try to drive it off on account of a miserable trickster who had a hand in all of this happening in the first place."

The little guy flinched and tried to hide behind my leg again. I tried to shake him off, but he just held on to my jeans even more tightly. Finally, I just looked down at him, meeting those beady, inhuman eyes. "If you keep holding on to me, you'll just get dragged to wherever that other thing is," I said. That did the trick. He let go and cowered in the corner as Dan stepped to the door and opened it.

"Are we actually going to drive this thing off?" I murmured to Dan.

"If we can," he said, "though that's usually a priest's bailiwick. If it's manifesting physically and trying to hurt people, we might be able to do something, even if it's only to discourage it." He didn't stop scanning the hallway in front of us. It just looked as dark, shabby, and abandoned as it had on the way in. "Be prepared for anything. From that little display earlier, this thing is pretty potent. It can throw a lot of nastiness at us between here and the lobby."

He stepped into the hallway. Nothing happened. I followed. Still nothing.

The door slammed shut behind us. I jumped; I was already a little keyed up, and now I was starting to wonder if this thing was going to come through a wall and grab me. Dan was facing down the hall, so I sort of instinctively covered the other direction, trying to look everywhere at once, almost more afraid that I was going to see something than that I was going to miss it. As weird as some of the stuff I'd seen with paranormal investigators and occultists over the last year had been, somehow I now felt like a kid trying not to look in the shadowy corner of his room, certain that the monster in the dark is there, watching him.

I almost didn't hear it at first. It was a low whispering, just below the range where you can make out words. It sounded like somebody was just on the other side of the wall, stage whispering. Even after I noticed it, I couldn't be sure I was actually hearing it. "Dan…"

"Yeah, I hear it," he said. He sighed. "So, it's going to be like that."

I started to ask what he meant, but he forged ahead. "Don't listen to it. Tune it out. It's going to start getting in your head. Keep focused and start praying. Prayer is poison to these things. It'll keep it from getting its claws in your head." He started moving toward the lobby. "Be ready for things to get plenty weird before we get out of here."

The whispering was getting louder and more insistent. The words were filled with hate, blasphemy, and despair. I quickly tried to do just what Dan had said, tune them out. I started to pray the Our Father and Hail Mary over and over, just trying to drown out the whispers.

Of course, that just meant it escalated.

Every door along the hallway slammed open and then shut again. The whispers turned to shouts, a blast of noise that seemed like it should have knocked us off our feet, except there still wasn't a breath of wind in the hall. The shouting and roaring became incomprehensible, nothing but a blast of rage and hate, which in a way I suppose was a blessing.

Dan tugged on my arm, and I followed him toward the door to the lobby. I kept one eye back down the hall, which was when I saw the apparition.

It was just a shape, at first. It looked like a man, but somehow...off. Unable to turn away, I looked closer, and saw that it looked strange because the man's neck was stretched and crooked...like he'd been hanged. If I'd been scared before, now I was positively petrified.

With jerky, unnatural movements, the figure walked toward us, looking almost like a stop-motion animation in an old movie. That was when I saw that it was John, his neck broken, his eyes gouged out, and screaming the hate and filth that the demon was bellowing from every corner of the hallway.

I must have made a noise, or stopped moving. Dan was suddenly beside me, speaking directly into my ear. "That's not your friend," he told me urgently. "It's trying to get to you. Fight it." He reached into his shirt, pulled out a small, intricately worked silver crucifix, kissed it, and let it hang on his chest. He addressed the figure that was still jerkily advancing on us. "You have no power here," he said. "I am a servant of God, and I command you back into the Abyss, scavenger, abomination, traitor." As he spoke, he leveled that hand cannon, but before he could fire, the apparition disappeared.

I started to breathe a little easier, but Dan pulled on my arm. "Come on. It's not done yet." I realized I was gripping the grip of my 1911 so hard that my hand hurt.

"Shooting these things works?" I asked.

23

"It helps," he replied as he led the way toward the lobby. "Bullets alone won't do the trick; I'll fill you in all the way when and if we get out of here."

"If?" I gulped.

He glanced back at me, for the first time since the demon had announced its presence. "You didn't think this was a risk-free job, did you?"

The whispers were back, and they were nastier than before. I hadn't thought that was possible, but the things they were saying were enough to give a grown man screaming nightmares. You think you've seen evil, until you hear the thoughts of a demon and realize that the crap you've seen is playground bully level.

I didn't know how Dan could be so calm. I was forcing myself to keep moving, trying to keep from turning into a shaking ball of fear and bile on the floor. I'd never been so scared in my life. I think it was his unshakeable assurance that got me through the next few minutes.

The door to the lobby was standing slightly ajar. As Dan reached for it, it slammed shut. Through my shaking terror, it struck me that this thing seemed to really like doing that.

Dan tried to open it. It was stuck fast. Then things got really ugly.

The whispering got louder. It was a full volume voice, as if the thing was talking to us from arm's distance away, but it was everywhere. It had become very matter-of-fact, telling us in great detail how it was going to kill us, then what it was going to do to us in the Abyss after it had forced us to blaspheme against God before we died. I nearly puked from the sheer vileness of it all, never mind the fear.

Dan gripped my arm. It steadied me a bit. Then he apparently decided the thing wasn't pissed off enough yet.

"Oh, shut up," he barked. "You're pathetic. Threats and noises in the dark. That's it? That little toad who was haunting this place before you got here is more dangerous than you. You know why? Because you've already lost, and you know it. The Pit's waiting for you regardless, and God isn't going to let you drag us down with you. So get lost!"

To my complete lack of surprise, that didn't go over very well. There was another roar of rage and hate that seemed to shake the entire motel, and almost drove me to my knees, but Dan's grip kept me upright. "Don't show fear," he said quietly, barely audible over the screaming. "Pray, and get ready to fight."

I did as he said. I think I must have said the Our Father about five times in as many breaths. It settled me down, and I stood straighter, flexing my hand around the grip of my 1911. Dan let go of my arm. "Now get ready. It's going to escalate things again."

Sure enough, a moment later the floor at the end of the hall seemed to crumble away, and a pair of too-long, skeletal arms came out of the hole. The taloned hands gripped the floor and pulled the shape of the thing up into the hall.

It was roughly man-shaped, but the proportions were all wrong, distorted and twisted like something in a funhouse mirror. One arm was longer than the other, one hand had four fingers, the other had seven. One leg was gimpy and skinny, the other was almost twice as thick, with talons in place of a foot. The thing's neck seemed too long, and the head was a skull-like horror with too many sharp teeth and too many eyes. In spite of the darkness, it was perfectly visible, which I took to mean that it wanted us to see it.

I kept murmuring the Pater Noster under my breath, and, somewhat to my surprise, I found I wasn't all that scared of this thing anymore. Almost as one, Dan and I lifted our pistols and opened fire.

It screamed as we shot it, though the bullets ripped straight through it and into the wall behind. Both of us were shouting the prayers now, though Dan had gone into what sounded a lot like some sort of exorcism. I couldn't really hear either one of us over the thunder of gunfire, and the concussions of the .45 and .44 in that hallway were downright painful. I was going to have some more permanent ringing in my ears after this.

I took a step forward as the slide locked back empty. Instinctively, not missing a beat of the prayer, I dropped the mag and snatched a spare one out of my back pocket, slamming it home and yanking the slide. Dan was right beside me as I leveled the pistol and commenced hammering more rounds into the thing, which was now shrinking back, screaming in pain. I still didn't know what was doing the trick; our gunfire didn't seem to be doing any physical damage, but it was acting like it was. Maybe it was the prayer, maybe it was the gunfire, maybe it was both. I didn't ask questions. I just kept shooting it, and kept praying. I was convinced that if I let up on either, it would get up and tear my head off.

Dan reloaded faster than I'd ever seen anyone reload a revolver. Two flicks of the wrist and it was done and that cannon was back up. He bellowed, seemingly louder than even the reports of both our pistols, "I banish you back to the Pit! In Nomine Patris, et Filii, et Spiritus Sancti!" He punctuated the command with a bullet to the thing's head.

Even as he fired, with one last, ear-splitting shriek, the thing dissolved into oily smoke and sank back through the floor. The hole it had ripped was gone as though it had never existed.

I'd fired my last round just as the thing disappeared. I stood there, my ears ringing painfully, breathing hard, staring at the spot where it had stood. I reloaded without even thinking about it, slamming my last spare mag in and sending the slide home mechanically. I still couldn't quite wrap my brain around what had just happened.

Dan's hand on my shoulder slightly shook me out of my reverie. "You did good, kid," he said. "I might not have to bury you early, after all. Come on, we've got places to be."

Chapter 3

We didn't stick around very long. Even as isolated as the abandoned motel was, somebody was bound to have heard the shooting, if not the howling and screaming. We didn't especially want to be around when the local sheriff's department showed up to find us and a bunch of bullet holes in an otherwise abandoned building. It probably wouldn't be taken as anything more serious than a couple of drunken rednecks shooting up an abandoned building, but Dan didn't want to deal with even that much, and I tended to agree.

Dan sprinkled holy water on the doorframes and the floor in the murder/suicide room, while I picked up brass. That wasn't so much to keep us from being identified, but because brass is reusable, and as Dan explained, nobody in this line of work is exactly swimming in money. By the time he'd finished his work, hopefully barring the demon from returning, I had all the brass in a plastic bag from the back of the Bronco and we were ready to go. We were about a half a mile down the highway before we saw the flashing lights of a sheriff's car heading toward the hotel.

"That was quick," I commented, as the green-and-black car sped by us.

"Well, considering that the hotel was just recently the scene of a murder-suicide, they can't very well ignore reports of shots fired coming from it, can they?" Dan pointed out. "They'll find nothing but bullet holes, and report it as vandalism, but without putting eyes on the scene, they don't know that." He chuckled. "Trust me; you get pretty good at predicting the police mindset in this business. Every once in a while, you'll meet a cop who's seen enough weird stuff to listen, but most of the time we've got to lay low and get gone as soon as the smoke clears."

"Have you ever been arrested doing this?" I asked.

"A couple of times," he said. "The first time I didn't get away fast enough after I got in a scrap with a goathead. I shot it, it ran, then the cops showed up. There wasn't a body, no particular damage to anything, so I got charged for discharging a firearm within city limits. Lost the rifle for two months. When the goathead came back, I had to finish it with my pistol, and that time there were witnesses. Nobody wanted to admit that it was a man with a goat's head and legs, so it got put down simply as 'self-defense,' and I got my rifle back and the earlier charge dismissed.

"The second time was hairier. I shot a man. Fortunately for me, he was trying to stab a girl with an obsidian knife. Had to go through the whole investigation, but got cleared and even declared a hero for saving the girl. According to the papers, he was just a serial killer wannabe, but the fact of the matter was, he had gone so bad that if I hadn't shot him then, things would have gotten really weird and really dangerous in that county for a long time."

He stared ahead at the road and the wheat fields rolling by. "That's something you're going to have to deal with," he said quietly. "Eventually, you're going to have to make the call, and you might have to drop the hammer on someone before they open a door that can't be closed. The powers of the Abyss are legion, they are full of hate so intense it could burn you to ash where you stand, and they are far smarter and more powerful than any man. If someone is summoning a demon, you'll have to do whatever it takes to stop them. And you'll have to live with the consequences of that action."

I didn't have a reply to that. The next few miles went by in silence, as I stared out the window and once again contemplated just what I'd gotten myself into.

The sun was starting to dip toward the horizon when we turned off the highway and onto a winding gravel road. "Timed that just about perfectly," Dan said, sounding pleased with himself. "We'll get to Ray's place just in time for dinner."

"Who's Ray?" I asked.

"Ray was a Hunter for a long time," Dan said, as we wound along the road, the sun behind us shining gold through the cloud of dust his truck was kicking up. "He retired out to his family ranch about ten years ago, for reasons you don't need to know yet. He's still got his hand in the game; he just doesn't go out himself anymore. He'll be happy to have us, and he might have a few more pointers for you that I might not have thought of just yet."

We slowly rolled up to the ranch house. It was a long, one-story log house, with lights in the windows as the sun went down. It sat nestled back in the trees, which were just starting to turn yellow and orange as fall approached. There was a barn and a corral just outside the treeline, but the corral looked like it was empty and hadn't been used for a long time. An ancient-looking 1950s Chevy pickup sat in front of the ranch house porch. Dan drove up next to it and parked. An enormous, shaggy dog was lying on the porch, and lifted its head to look at us as we got out.

I kind of hung back as Dan walked up onto the porch, extending his hand to the dog. "Hey, Magnus," he said quietly. The enormous canine sniffed his hand and *whuffed* a greeting, his tail wagging, thumping against the wall. Dan scratched him behind the ears as the door opened.

The man standing in the doorway was probably one of the biggest men I've ever seen. He had to stand almost seven feet tall, with longish white hair and a white ZZ Top beard that flowed down over a barrel chest. His arms and hands looked like he could bend I-beams. There was a leather holster at his side, with what looked like an old, stainless Smith and Wesson semi-auto in it. "Howdy, Dan," he drawled. "Figured it was you when Magnus didn't start barking as soon as your truck door slammed." He held out an enormous hand, and Dan stood up from where he was petting Magnus to shake it. The handshake turned into a bearhug.

"I've missed you, old man," Dan said.

29

"It's been too long," Ray agreed. He jerked his head toward me, his beard wagging. As soon as Dan had stopped scratching his ears, Magnus had come down off the porch to give me a sniff. The dog was even bigger than I'd thought. "Who's the kid?"

Dan looked back at me. "This is Jed," he said. "I've taken him under my wing. He's done okay so far."

Ray stepped down off the porch to offer his hand. My own disappeared into that huge mitt. He studied me for a second. His eyes were brown, shaded in a maze of squint lines. His scrutiny was a little unnerving. Aside from his sheer size, there was a sense of quiet intensity about the man that was intimidating, and even back then, I didn't get intimidated easily.

"This is the young feller you were looking for, isn't he?" Ray asked Dan, still studying me. "The one linked to those killings?"

Dan nodded, leaning against one of the posts that held the porch roof up. "The same. Turns out he had a bit of an encounter out in the sandbox, and got in over his head looking for answers. He's come around."

Ray continued to look me over for a few moments before he nodded, apparently satisfied. "Where you boys headed?" he asked.

"Colorado," I said. "It turns out I've got some unfinished business back there."

Ray raised an eyebrow, but otherwise didn't comment. I had a feeling that the older man wasn't the type to say much about what he was told until he'd had time to go over it in his head. "Well, come on in," he said. "I'll put a couple more steaks on."

We followed him inside, Magnus padding after us. The ranch house had a warm, homey feel, the kind of place I hadn't seen in a long, long time. The walls were some kind of blond wood, and the floor was flat stone. A large fireplace dominated the slightly sunken living room, which opened onto the kitchen and dining table. There was a fire crackling in the fireplace. Several sets of very impressive antlers were mounted above the mantel, around and below a large, ornate crucifix. The rest of that wall was covered by bookcases, all of them full to overflowing. A couple of comfortable couches were set facing the fireplace in a sort of V, and several rugs were thrown over the stone floor. Both couches had deerskins draped over the backs.

The kitchen table was a big, solid wood affair that looked like it could seat at least eight people. There were only two sturdy wooden chairs pulled up to it at the moment, but just judging from the look of the rest of the place, Ray could easily pull several more out of a back room.

"You get a lot of visitors?" I asked as he went into the kitchen and pulled a paper-wrapped packet of meat out of the refrigerator.

He chuckled. "Oh, yeah. This is sort of a way-station for members of the Order. Any Hunter is welcome here, any time. Dan's spent more time here than anywhere else in the last twenty years." He walked to the fireplace, where I noticed he had a grate set up over the flames, and tossed the steaks on, next to the one he already had cooking. I hadn't seen many people cook in their fireplace, but I liked it. It added to the down-home, frontier feel of the place. He went back into the kitchen, wrapped a couple of potatoes in foil, and shoved them into the coals as well.

Ray motioned for us to have a seat on one of the couches, and we obliged, accepting the dark brown bottles he fetched from the fridge. Magnus settled down on a well-worn rug by the fire, panting as he watched the steaks sizzle. I opened the flip top cap on the bottle and took a sip. It was some of the richest, best-tasting beer I think I'd ever tasted, and that included times when I hadn't just about had my head ripped off by a demon.

Ray settled himself on the other couch, leaning back in the cushions and sipping a beer of his own. He still hadn't taken off the pistol; I realized that neither Dan nor I had put ours aside, either. He and Dan chatted about the ranch, hunting, fishing, and what was going on with several people I'd never heard of. I noticed that they never ventured into the subject of the supernatural or fighting it. Dan hadn't even mentioned the encounter in the old motel. I was momentarily content to go along, and sat sipping my beer, watching the fire and Magnus, who had put his massive head down on his equally huge paws, and was watching us quietly.

It didn't take long before Ray was flipping the steaks out of the fire and onto plates. He rolled the potatoes out, and we moved over to the table.

The steaks weren't beef. They were venison, and pretty fresh from the taste. I hadn't had venison in a long time. I was finding I didn't want to leave this place.

The dinner conversation continued as before, but once we got up, cleared the plates away, and moved to the porch, things got serious again.

"So, tell me about this unfinished business in Colorado," Ray said.

Dan nodded to me, so I haltingly described my involvement. "I was hanging out with a group of paranormal investigators out in South Dakota," I explained, "the Piedmont Ghost Hunters. I'd seen enough of their stuff to think they might have seen some actual paranormal stuff, so I went out there to look them up. They didn't have much in the way of investigations going at the time; it's something they do about once every month or two. But they told me about this little college in Colorado, called Howard Philips College. They said it had a full-time paranormal/occult studies department, and that if I had questions about the supernatural, I should go there and look up Professor Clark Ashton.

"I didn't feel like waiting around until their next little outing, so I hit the road for Colorado. It took a week to arrange a meeting with Ashton; either he's a really popular guy, or he likes to keep people waiting to make it seem that way."

"Did he live up to his reputation?" Ray asked. He was just sitting there on his porch swing, one hand stroking that enormous beard, staring out at the corral as the light faded.

"I guess," I said. "I didn't have much of a yardstick to measure against at the time; I guess I still don't, not really. He had a lot of books, a lot of stories, and a lot of videos that *looked* authentic. He asked me all sorts of questions about the fight with the…ifrit out in the desert, recorded the interviews and everything. But he never told me what it was. Come to think of it, he never told me all that much; he just invited me to join his little club. He had an exclusive study group of students; I never met them, but from what I heard, they were pretty hard-core fans of his."

"Why didn't you take him up on the invitation?" Ray was still staring thoughtfully at the darkening meadow.

32

"I don't know," I said. "I guess I wasn't all that interested in joining anybody at the time. I felt like I had to keep moving." I frowned. "Kinda weird, now that I think about it."

Neither of the others commented, so I continued on. "After a while, I got restless. I still hadn't gone through all of his books; I think that would take several years of non-stop reading. But I just didn't feel like I was getting any answers, and Ashton just kept urging me to take his classes and join his little circle of students. So I left."

"And something followed you." Ray finally looked over at Dan. "What was it?"

Dan shook his head. "Don't know. I haven't seen it; in fact, nobody has that I know of who's lived to tell about it. There was a Nimerigar or something like that in the motel where Samuels and his friends were killed. It was the one creating the 'haunting.'" Ray grunted, sounding vaguely annoyed. Dan ignored it. "It said that something had come, that it smelled wrong, and that it murdered those kids. Said it 'smelled like smoke and fire.'"

Ray frowned. "Demonic?"

Dan shook his head. "Even a Nimerigar would know a demon; it would have said so. It didn't know what it was. But here's the thing; whatever it was, it left a mark on the wall, *under* the wallpaper. And it was a mark that Jed here recognized from one of Ashton's books."

Ray's eyes narrowed. He rocked back in the swing, thinking, absently scratching behind Magnus' ears. The big dog had come out and hopped up on the swing next to him.

"There are a few things out there that will do that," he said after a long moment. "But without more to go on…"

He stopped talking as Magnus' head came up. The dog stared toward the trees and growled. It was the deepest, probably scariest noise I think I've ever heard a dog make.

Dan and Ray were on their feet in an instant. "You got a long gun, kid?" Ray asked me.

I shook my head, straining my eyes in the direction Magnus was staring. The big, bear-like dog was off the swing now, facing the treeline and downright bristling, his fangs exposed as he continued to growl. "I had an AR a couple years ago, but I had to sell it a few months back. All I've got now is my 1911."

Dan was already heading down to his truck. Ray shook his head. "Not gonna be enough in this business. Come with me." He led the way back inside and into a hallway that stretched back from the dining room.

He took out a key to open a small room at the very back. As the door swung open, I saw that it was steel, set in a steel frame, bolted to thick logs. Nobody was getting into that room without either the key or some serious breaching tools.

Ray flicked on a light, and if it hadn't been for the very real and immediate threat just outside, I would have started salivating. It was an arms room, and a pretty well stocked one. The rifles on the racks against the wall were mostly older bolt-actions and lever guns, with a handful of modern semi-autos. Ray looked at me appraisingly, then went over and picked up one of the lever-actions.

"How well can you work a lever gun?" he asked.

"It's been a while, but I'd say I'm decent with one," I said.

He nodded, and handed me the rifle. It was far from new; the wood was worn and shiny, and there was a faint patina on the steel. But when I cycled the action, it was smooth as butter. Someone had taken very good care of this gun. I didn't immediately recognize the action, but engraved on the back strap of the receiver, stretching down onto the stock, it said, "Model 1886, Winchester Trade Mark."

"I know you're probably more comfortable with semi-autos," he said, as he handed me a bandolier of rounds each almost the size of my thumb, "but they don't make semis in .45-70. And believe me, kid; against some of the things you're going to meet, you want a gun that throws *really* big bullets. Since I don't have any elephant guns, this is the next best thing."

I just nodded my thanks, as I slung the bandolier over my shoulder and started shoving gigantic cartridges into the rifle's loading port. I'd fired some big stuff, including .45-70, before, but never in combat. This was going to be interesting.

Even from inside the arms room, we could still hear Magnus. He was barking now, deep, threatening barks that echoed menacingly off the trees and the hills. The noise seemed

34

to vibrate inside my chest with every bark. There was something extraordinary about that dog.

Ray had picked up a heavy-barreled, bolt-action carbine with a box magazine, and was shoving more .45-70 cartridges into the mag as we made our way back out to the porch.

Dan was standing by the truck, just off the porch, with his .50 Beowulf in hand. Magnus hadn't moved, but was barking his displeasure toward the trees.

Standing in the treeline was a figure.

It wasn't large; I figured it stood about five feet tall at most. It was shaped like a man, but its head was too big. I couldn't make out much detail in the light coming from the windows, except for a too-wide slash of a mouth and a pair of dark, glittering eyes.

As soon as I saw it, I noticed a strange smell in the air. It was vaguely sour, kind of like stale vomit. It didn't bode well, and I suspected it had something to do with the weird thing in the trees.

It started to walk toward us, with a sort of jerky movement that didn't look at all natural. It almost looked like a marionette skipping across the clearing toward us. None of us had to say anything. Magnus was getting more agitated, his barks even more threatening than before, if that was possible. Almost as one, the three of us shouldered our rifles and opened fire.

I hadn't had a chance to zero the Winchester, obviously, but I found I trusted that Ray had made sure it was set up right, and I needn't have worried. I put the gold bead front sight on the advancing creature and fired. I hadn't put any earplugs in, so the thundering concussion of two .45-70s and a .50 set my ears to ringing immediately, but I saw the thing stagger under the impact of three massive bullets.

It didn't stop, though. It just shook itself, seemed to grin wider, and kept coming.

Dan was shooting faster than either Ray or I, but not by much. I worked the lever and put another round into the thing, making it sway with the impact but not much more than that. Dan was already moving off to the thing's flank, keeping up steady fire, and I stepped off the porch, trying to spread out. I didn't know exactly what good it would do; I doubted the thing had a hand grenade that could take us all out if we bunched up, but at the time, it seemed like the right thing to do.

The thunder of our gunfire was rolling echoes off the hills now. The thing still hadn't made a sound, just slowly advanced with that creepy, imbecilic grin on its otherwise featureless face. It was getting close enough now that even in the low light, I put the gold bead on its head and squeezed off another round.

Its head rocked back, and I thought I saw a wound pucker in the thing's face, but it just kept coming, seemingly unfazed. It wasn't moving at more than a slow walk, but unless we could kill it, that was going to be small comfort.

"Keep your distance!" Ray yelled from the porch as he worked the bolt on his carbine. "Don't let it get within arm's reach of you!" He shot it again, with just as little effect as before.

"What the hell is it?" I all but screamed as I put another shot into it. It had paused at the corner of the porch and was looking back and forth at us, as though trying to decide which one of us to go after first. That was when I saw the wisdom of spreading out.

It stared at me as I backed away, shoving more cartridges into the rifle's loading port. I wasn't sure how many shots I'd fired; facing the creepiness of that thing had me rattled. I just knew that it hadn't gone *click* when I pulled the trigger yet, and I didn't want to get to that point. It looked at me again as I found I couldn't get another round in the tube, then started toward Dan. I whipped the rifle to my shoulder again and shot it, rocking its head to the side but otherwise doing nothing.

"Shooting it isn't working!" I was starting to freak out a little. I glanced over at Dan, who seemed to be speaking, though I couldn't make out what he was saying. Then I realized I'd gotten so focused on shooting that I'd forgotten the prayer component that Dan had told me about. But it didn't seem to be slowing down for anything.

Then I noticed that Ray wasn't shooting anymore. I glanced up toward the porch, where Magnus was standing in front of the door, continuing to bark, though his barks now seemed muted next to the hammering of heavy-caliber rifle shots. Ray was nowhere to be seen.

The thing was continuing to advance on Dan, driving him back toward the road. I was shouting the Our Father at the top of

36

my lungs now, but it didn't seem to be doing much. I didn't get it. Nothing was working.

Ray came striding out of the barn, walking quickly toward the thing. He had a lit weed burner in his hands.

Both Dan and I stopped shooting as Ray walked toward it. It seemed to stay focused on Dan for a moment, before it looked back and saw Ray, and the big propane torch roaring toward its face.

For the first time, the thing moved quickly. It still didn't make a sound, but turned and ran for the trees, with the same weird, disjointed puppet gait it had walked out of them with. In moments it was out of sight.

There wasn't much hesitation once it was gone. The echoes of gunfire and Magnus' barking had barely faded before Ray was putting the weed burner back in the barn, lifting a lantern, and motioning to us to follow him. He didn't say a word, but led the way into the woods, in a different direction than that whatever-it-was had gone.

The woods got thick fast; there was the gurgle of a stream in back of the house, and there were the requisite birches, aspens, and similar river-bottom trees growing along the banks and extending on up the hill. Ray lit the lantern a few steps into the trees, for which I was grateful. While it might show that thing where we were, the light would also hopefully keep it from sneaking up on us. I found that I could see a long way by the light it cast, as long as I didn't look directly at the lantern itself, or even too close to it.

He led the way over a small wooden bridge that crossed the stream. It looked like there was a well-worn path leading back into the woods. I wondered if there was another barn or something back there.

What it led to wasn't a barn, or any structure at all, really. It led into a grove of big, gnarled trees and simply stopped. Ray stepped into the center of the grove, set the lantern on the ground, leaned against a tree, and waited. Since he wasn't saying anything, and neither was Dan, I decided that silence was probably the best choice, and settled in to wait. At that point, I had pretty much resigned myself to just seeing what happened next. It was almost guaranteed to be weird, and I'd learn a lot more by just keeping my mouth shut and watching and listening.

For a long time nothing happened. The lantern hissed, and the night breeze sighed through the upper branches. A couple of the trees creaked, and several nocturnal animals shuffled in the undergrowth and fallen leaves. None of us moved, or said anything. Both Dan and Ray appeared to be waiting for something in particular.

Finally, Ray shoved off of the tree he'd been leaning against. I looked around, and saw a faint glimmer through the trees, getting closer. The glimmer eventually resolved itself into a figure, walking through the forest.

As she—and she was definitely a she, no doubt about that —stepped into the little glade, I saw that she wasn't so much glowing, as she was somehow illuminated, even though everything else outside of the lantern's small circle of light was now pitch dark. It was as if there was a spotlight shining on just her, but kind of a golden one.

I finally got a good look at her, and she was breathtaking. Willow-slender, but rounded in all the right places, with hair down to her thighs, that seemed to shimmer between spun gold, coppery red, and deep brown, depending on how the source-less light seemed to hit it. She was dressed in a simple white, sleeveless gown, belted at the waist, which covered her while falling in just the right way to accentuate every curve.

Her face and eyes, though, were even more captivating. Her features were the most delicately shaped I'd ever seen. Her face was heart-shaped, with a slightly pointed chin and thin, slightly up-turned nose. Her eyes, though…her eyes were slightly slanted, and her irises were gold. Not light brown, but gold, like a wolf's.

Those golden eyes were fixed on me, and her full, red lips were curved up in a smile that seemed at once promising and predatory. I think I might have been drooling a little at that point, up until Dan's callused hand connected firmly with the back of my head.

"Keep your head clear, kid," he growled, as I rubbed the base of my skull. It hadn't been a gentle smack. The apparition of a woman swayed her way across the glade, barely seeming to touch the ground, her eyes still fixed on me, though her lips had drooped in a pout.

"Oh, Daniel," she said, her honeyed voice as enticing as the rest of her, "why must you be such a wet blanket?" She slid up to where she was almost touching me, looking up into my face. I was sweating now, and found myself trying hard to look at anything but those lambent golden eyes. "I'm just trying to say hello…" She was so close that I could feel her body heat. She smelled like spices and flowers. I was going to have to look at those eyes again soon, and then I'd be lost in them…

"That's enough, Fand," Ray snapped, his voice cracking harshly across the glade. "Back off the kid. We're here on business."

She pouted again, lifting her hand as if to touch my cheek, but drawing back just short. "There's no reason not to mix business and pleasure, Raymond," she said. "You bring me new people to meet so rarely…and such a beautiful young man even more rarely…" She smiled at me again as she stepped away, and I blew out a ragged breath.

"I said enough." Whether Ray was just used to her or preternaturally composed, I didn't know, but I envied him his assurance. I was actually shaking worse than I had been after leaving the demon-haunted Drop Inn. "You saw the thing that attacked us at the house?"

"Of course, darling," she purred. "I see everything that happens in these woods, you know that."

"What was it?" he asked flatly.

She looked over at me again, that heart-stopping little smile on her lips. "For a little time to get to know this beautiful boy, I'll tell you everything about it," she said. "Maybe even enough to catch it…"

"Forget it, Fand." Ray was starting to sound pissed, and Magnus growled, the first sound he'd made since we'd gotten to the glade. I glanced over to see the big dog staring at Fand, his jaws shut but his ruff bristling. There was a curious intensity to the dog's gaze. I was really starting to think that there was something very unusual about Magnus, but given everything else that was going on, that should come as no surprise. "Are you forgetting the terms of the agreement?"

She pouted even more, but by then even I could tell it was a put-on. With a theatrical sigh, she said, "Of course not, Raymond. I still owe you, so you may ask whatever questions you may like, and I will answer them, without further payment." She looked back at me through her lashes and sighed again. "The creature that attacked your house was a homunculus, and an exceptionally well made one. Obviously, I can't tell you what it was here for; it doesn't have a mind to read. Only puppet strings…and I cannot say where they lead. Not that I wouldn't love to tell you everything, my dear, but I simply cannot see where they go. They vanish quickly into a mist of confusion and deceit." For once, she seemed to get serious, letting the seductive act fall away. She was just as intoxicating, but she wasn't actively trying. "There is powerful sorcery at work here," she said. "I dare not get too close to it; it might claim me as well."

Ray frowned. I looked over at Dan, and he looked just as perturbed. At least I wasn't the only one who thought that sounded ominous.

"What's a homunculus?" I asked. Dan and Ray both looked over at me sharply, and Fand looked at me with a gleam in her eye that was at once enticing and scary as hell. Before she could say anything, though, Ray spoke.

"A homunculus is an artificial man," he said, "made through an alchemical mixture of clay, herbs, and human blood. They have no minds of their own, though sometimes they can be used as focuses for particularly powerful—and usually malign—spirits. It sounds like this one's being remote-controlled, though." He shot me a warning glance as he finished. I wasn't sure why, but apparently I'd stuck my foot in it by asking the question in the first place.

Fand nodded, with a regretful moue as she looked at me. I started to think that Ray had rescued me from something by answering the question before she could. "There is no spirit inhabiting this one, no," she said. "Like I said, puppet strings, leading off into the darkest night."

"Can you tell anything about these 'puppet strings'?" Ray asked.

She hesitated. For the first time that night, her seductive self-assurance seemed to falter. She looked down at the ground for the briefest moment. It struck me suddenly. This alien creature, whatever she was—and I was pretty sure by then that she wasn't human—was terrified. "I cannot. There is evil in those threads, an evil I can smell as surely as I can see you. If I get too close…" Her voice trailed off, and I could have sworn she shivered.

There was a long silence. Even Magnus seemed quieted. Finally, Ray said, "That is all we require of you tonight, Fand. You may go."

She sighed again, and looked at me one more time, this time with all the intoxicating sensuality she'd hit me with from the beginning. "Be sure to come back and see me soon, beautiful boy," she said, and blew me a kiss. My knees almost buckled. Then she swayed out of the glade and back into the trees. She was still visible, bathed in her own little glimmer of golden light, for some time before she faded into the forest.

Once she had vanished, Dan blew out a huge breath. Ray bent down and picked up the lantern. "I take it you didn't tell him about Fand?" he asked Dan.

Dan shook his head. "No, and that's my fault. Haven't had a new guy tagging along for too long." He turned to me. "You're very lucky that Ray answered your question before she had a chance to," he explained. "The Fae are very picky about debts; if she'd answered you, she'd have expected something in exchange, and you wouldn't get to pick what it was. They're tricky like that."

"So she was a fairy?" I asked. It said something about my life recently that that sounded like a perfectly rational question.

"Yes, she is," Ray said, "in the oldest and most dangerous sense of that word." He started back toward the house, with Magnus trotting at his heels. "They're rarely seen anymore, which tends to make people less leery of them. They aren't *evil*, strictly speaking, but they're no less dangerous to be around. They're weird and capricious, and they've got an odd sense of fun. They'll mess with your head and your life, but rarely out of actual malice, at least compared to some of the other things crawling around the Otherworld. Everything's a game to them, and humans make exceptionally entertaining playthings. I've rarely heard of a Fae killing a human, but more than one has had their life and sanity destroyed by their games."

He kept looking around the woods as we walked. Magnus seemed to be very alert, too. After everything that had happened that night, my senses were thrumming, as I tried to see and hear everything. "A few years before I retired, I found this old guy wandering around in Yellowstone, completely out of his head. Took him to the sheriff's office, and they had no idea who he was. Complete John Doe. Eventually we got a name out of him, and with some research found out he was a hiker who'd gone missing fifty years before. He'd stumbled onto a Fae's night picnic, and she treated him to her hospitality for half a century. He had no idea what was real and what wasn't anymore. No idea what he saw when he was a 'guest,' but it left him completely detached from this world." He glanced back at me. "Sometimes it can be advantageous to talk to them, but never, ever trust them. Always have some kind of leverage on a Fae before you ask them any questions."

"I guess you've got some pretty good leverage on her, then?" I said.

He just smiled slightly. "You could say that." He didn't elaborate, and I decided not to press the issue.

None of us said anything more before getting back to the house. Once we got there, I made to hand back the .45-70, but Ray waved me off. "Keep it," he said. "The guy who first carried it ain't coming back for it, and I think he'd be happy to see it getting some use again. I can give you a couple hundred rounds for it before you leave, too." He looked over at Dan. "That'll be in the morning, I take it?"

Dan nodded, sinking onto the couch with his big Beowulf AR across his knees. "After that little display, we need to get this nailed down quick," he said. "Somebody's messing around with some seriously bad medicine. We've got to stop it, hopefully before anybody else gets killed."

Ray stroked his beard. "Well, you boys better get some sleep, then," he said. "I'll stay up to get some things set up for you, and Magnus will let us know if that thing shows up again." He scratched the big dog behind the ears, and Magnus just about bowled him over with a shove against his legs. "I'll see you in the morning."

It took a while to get to sleep. Ray had several guest rooms in the house, and apparently three more in the loft in the barn. The bed was plenty comfortable, but the events of the last few days, especially the night's encounters, were weighing on my mind and made it hard to sleep.

After what felt like hours of tossing and turning, I finally faded out. Shortly thereafter, I seemed to wake up somewhere else.

It looked like a small, stone chapel, lit by candles and sunlight streaming through some of the most exquisite stained glass windows I've ever seen. The pews were old, dark wood, as was the altar as well as the crucifix above it. I walked down the narrow aisle toward the front, where a figure was sitting in the front pew.

He looked back as I approached. He was tall and lanky and looked about Ray's age, with white hair and a white mustache. He actually looked a lot like Sam Elliot. "Jed," he said by way of greeting. He waved a hand to the pew next to him. Taking it as an invitation, I genuflected in front of the altar and sat down.

"How did I get here?" I asked, when he didn't say anything right away.

He chuckled. "You haven't gone anywhere. You're still in bed, asleep," he said. "This is the best way for us to talk right now."

"Okay," I said. I'd seen enough weirdness recently to take that claim in stride, especially since it seemed to be the most logical explanation for why I didn't remember getting up and going to some small chapel somewhere. "So who are you?"

"I'm a friend," he said. "One you've always had, though you haven't always known it."

I squinted at him. He was being cryptic, but that seemed to be par for the course in this bizarre new life I'd stumbled into. "Are you trying to say you're my guardian angel, or something?"

He smiled beneath the mustache. "That's pretty much it, yeah," he drawled. "We don't usually talk directly with our charges, but you've become something of a special case."

I looked around the chapel. I didn't know what to think. It's not every day you have a vivid dream where someone or something claiming to be your guardian angel introduces himself.

I wasn't getting any sense of dread or threat, though, which I took to be a good sign.

"How so?" I asked, deciding to play along at least until I got a better feel for where the dream was going.

He raised his eyebrows. "Every mortal man faces a certain level of spiritual warfare in their lives. Unfortunately, a lot of them don't notice it or see it for what it is, and they lose. You, though…like your new brethren, you've stepped into the front lines in a way most people never even dream of." He stood up. "Your position means I get a little bit more leeway to contact and guide you. A little bit, mind you." He smiled slightly. "Most of my advice is still going to sound awfully cryptic, but that's the way the rules go. If I start getting too clear, you should probably start taking things very, very seriously."

I looked up him with a raised eyebrow of my own. "Are you saying this situation isn't that serious?"

"That's a rather relative thing," he said. "It's plenty serious, but it's not outside your ability to handle without me holding your hand. Trust me; you'll get to know what I'm talking about in good time. Don't rush it."

I didn't get a chance to ask any more questions before the chapel faded out and I opened my eyes on the faint, gray light of dawn leaking through the curtains.

Chapter 4

Howard Phillips College hadn't changed much since I'd been there the first time. Of course, it had only been a couple of months since I'd left it, so I don't know what I might have been expecting.

It wasn't a large campus, nor was it especially old. While a couple of the houses on the south side had been converted to the college's use and were almost a century old, most of the place had been built within the last thirty years.

The campus center was dominated by Phillips Hall, which, while it was only fifteen years old, had been built to look like an old-time university hall, with vaulted ceilings, a Greco-Roman columned portico, and high, arched windows. The wide, double mahogany doors opened on the grassy circle with a concrete fountain in the center that formed the heart of the campus. Also fronting on the circle were two lecture halls and the student union building. The lecture halls were built in the same style as Phillips Hall, but the student union building was a block of brick and glass that looked out of place. Strangely, it was five years older than any of the rest.

Dan had parked in the north lot, near the library, and we walked down to Phillips Hall. Neither of us was armed with anything but knives, holy water flasks, and crucifixes. Dan had explained that, barring some exceptional circumstances, the kind of fights we get into rarely happen during the day. I wasn't comfortable leaving my guns in the truck, but carrying concealed without a permit in Colorado was a good way to go to jail if something did pop off, and as Dan patiently pointed out, we weren't to the shooting phase with Professor Ashton yet.

I wanted to bring up the homunculus, but I realized I didn't know if anyone had yet seen it in daylight. We hadn't. And if Ashton had sent it, I doubted he'd necessarily want the added scrutiny of it tearing somebody apart in the middle of the day. He'd been a little weird when I'd talked to him, but he hadn't seemed creepy or malicious. If he was, in fact, a murderous, homunculus-controlling sorcerer, then he seemed to be trying to be low-key about it.

Maybe it was just the knowledge I had coming back, but the campus seemed somehow darker, more sinister, in spite of the bright, warm, if somewhat blustery, day. It was with a palpable sense of dread that I walked up to Phillips Hall, intending to go in and inquire after Professor Ashton. He'd been headquartered in one of the southern lecture halls the last time I'd been there, but I felt the need to check that he hadn't moved, for some reason.

Dan and I walked through the doors and into the Hall. The reception desk was right on the atrium, built out of the same mahogany as the doors. Howard Phillips wasn't a cheap school to go to, and it showed.

The pretty blond at the desk smiled up at me as I approached, though the expression was as vague and vacant as could be expected from anybody who has to smile at everyone who comes through the door for hours at a time. "Can I help you?" she asked.

"I'm looking for Professor Clark Ashton," I said.

Just for a second, her fixed smile slipped. It was the briefest of flickers, barely even a change of expression, really, but I'd seen it. I couldn't tell if it was fear or distaste, and I didn't comment. I just filed the observation away for later.

She reached for a campus map on the desk and handed it to me. "He has recently moved to the Feist House, on the south side of campus," she said, her tone noticeably cooler than her initial greeting. "I believe he's living there as well as having his office and his classes there, so if you go knock on the door you should find him. Are you a student?"

"No, I'm not," I answered honestly. "I can't afford to enroll here. But I met the Professor a few months ago, and I had some more questions for him."

Her scrutiny was even cooler now. I guessed that Ashton's fascinations didn't necessarily go over that well with everyone else on campus. I decided to probe her a little bit. "You don't seem like a fan of his," I ventured.

She sniffed slightly. "I'm not," she said, "which would make me something of a minority around here. And if you wouldn't mind, I'm not in the mood for another lecture about what an eccentric genius he is."

I kept my expression under control. I knew that I should leave her out of this, but if she was somebody who already didn't like Ashton, I might get some useful information out of her, information that one of his little circle wouldn't necessarily give out. "I wasn't going to. I only met with him briefly…I'm just curious, is all. Why don't you like him?"

She raised an eyebrow and snorted a little. "That should be obvious to anyone with any common sense," she said, all trace of the friendly, cheerful receptionist gone. "This is a school, and he's turning a bunch of the students into a clique of occultist whackos. Nobody with half a brain believes this kind of stuff, but he's got them eating it up, wasting their time with ghosts and spirits and nonsense like that. It's about sensationalism and his little groupies, not learning. He's a fraud and a con artist. Does that answer your question?"

Actually it did, including the ones I hadn't asked. She didn't believe that there were any things that go bump in the night, so if Ashton really was into the dark, sinister stuff, she'd dismiss it all as a con anyway. The fact that he apparently had a large and growing following among the students was an interesting bit of information, however.

With a nod, I replied, "It does. And I understand. I'd be skeptical too, if I hadn't seen the things I have. I'll try to keep an open mind."

She rolled her eyes, and pointed to the square on the map that represented the Feist House. "Whatever. The house is there. If you want to waste your time, go ahead. It's none of my business, anyway." She turned her attention back to her tablet, apparently deciding that I wasn't worth any more of her attention. Rather unprofessional, but I wasn't going to make an issue out of it.

"Thank you," I said, getting a somewhat derisive sniff in return. Taking the map, I turned and headed back out the doors.

Dan was waiting, leaning against one of the columns. "He's still here?" he asked.

I nodded, holding up the map. "He's got new digs; apparently he moved into one of the older houses down on the south side of campus. He's living and working out of the Feist House now."

Dan's eyes narrowed, deepening the creases around them. "Feist? That name sounds familiar..."

"I'm guessing not in a good way, either, from the way you're frowning," I said, as we walked back down the steps to the sidewalk.

"If it's what I'm thinking, no. It's not." He kept looking around, that same frowning squint going on. "Damn. I don't remember for sure, and I don't exactly have a copy of the archives in the truck. I'll have to call somebody and get them to do some digging. It's niggling at the back of my brain, though..." He trailed off, continuing to study the campus as we walked.

The Feist House was at the far south side of the campus, one of the old houses on the far side of Higgins Road that the college had scooped up in an expansion a few years before. It was shrouded in trees, mostly aspens and old, gnarled oaks, and there was a thick hedge around most of it, that had been trimmed down to waist height at the gate.

The house itself was pure faux-Victorian. It was two stories, with a deep, shadowed porch and the requisite turreted tower. It looked like a repainted haunted house. It fit the whole "gothic occultist" thing Ashton had going to a tee.

"I'll stay out here, go for another turn around the campus," Dan said as I stepped up to the wrought-iron gate. "It'll be best if he thinks you're alone. He finds out that you're roaming around with an old fart like me, he might start asking questions."

"What if it's not him?" I asked. "What if it's a student?"

He shrugged. "Doesn't matter. Same principle applies. Never give up an advantage you don't have to, and having another gun in the shadows that nobody knows about is an advantage."

Dan was talking sense, as much as I really didn't want to go in there by myself. I think he sensed my hesitation, too. "You were a Marine, and you did pretty good against the demon in the Drop Inn and that homunculus at Ray's place. You'll be fine. Say a prayer before you go in, and keep your eyes open. If things start getting weird, get out and meet me by the fountain."

I nodded reluctantly and turned to the gate, as Dan continued down the sidewalk. I studied the house as I opened the gate, but didn't see anyone in the darkened windows. With everything else painting such a near-perfect gothic picture, I'd expected the gate to creak ominously as I opened it, but it swung open smoothly and silently on well-oiled hinges. I made my way up the walk to the porch. The yard was well-kept, and the trees had been recently pruned.

The front door had been painted a dark green, and had a snarling gargoyle knocker on it. I took a deep breath and knocked.

It took long enough that I was about to knock again when the door swung open. Ashton was standing there, and after a moment, his face lit up in a wide smile. "Jed! You came back! I was hoping you would. Come in, come in." He ushered me inside.

The foyer opened up on the living room. For some reason, I was struck by the contrast with Ray's place. Everything was much more refined, with a dark, ebony mantelpiece, richly upholstered chairs and couches built apparently of the same wood, a fine wood and glass coffee table, and every bit of wall space taken up by book and display cases. The contents of the display cases made me a little uneasy; they were mostly talismans and other occult artifacts. The place was like a Halloween store, except I had no doubt, after my previous meetings with Ashton, that they were genuine, or at least as genuine as he could get.

Ashton was a small man, maybe five-foot-six and thin enough that he looked almost waifish. He had a wide forehead, with thinning, flyaway hair, perpetually sunken cheeks and eyes, and a thin mustache that looked like it belonged in the thirties.

Every time I'd seen him, he was wearing what looked like the same rumpled white shirt and faded blazer with dark brown elbow patches, and this time was no exception. "Here, have a seat," he said, pointing to one of the chairs. "Can I get you something? Coffee, or a Coke?"

I sat down, shaking my head. I hadn't been sure what to expect, especially if he'd sent the homunculus after me, but he seemed to be just as friendly and personable as he'd been the last time I'd been there. "No, thank you," I said. Looking around, I recognized a number of the books on the shelves from his previous library, though none of the really heavy ones he'd let me look at. I guessed those were for special cases, and not anything he wanted casual visitors to see that he had.

He sat down across from me, perched on the edge of a couch like a nervous bird. He put his elbows on his knees and folded his hands. "So," he said, eagerly, "have you found out anything new since you left?"

Plenty, I thought, but I shook my head. "Not really. Just more people without any real idea of what they're looking for, stumbling around in the dark looking for ghosts. It wasn't really any help. The only time I seemed to find any solid information was here, in your library."

He nodded. "A lot of people are interested in the paranormal and the occult, but don't do enough research before investigating it firsthand," he said. "It can be quite dangerous for the uninitiated."

It was a struggle not to raise an eyebrow at his use of the word *uninitiated*, but I managed to keep my expression pretty blank.

"So, you've come back to study more?" His eagerness was almost painful. "You'll reconsider my offer to join our little study group?"

I nodded slowly. "I'm still not enrolled as a student or anything," I ventured. "I can't really afford it."

He waved his hand, smiling widely. "Not an issue, especially not in the case of someone who's had as close a brush with the paranormal as you have. You're more than welcome to sit in on my classes and work with us, student status or not. You won't get any college credit for it, of course, but that doesn't seem to be something you're all that worried about."

I shook my head. It wasn't.

"As it turns out, you're just in time," he said. "We're about to start the fall semester, and I've got a new class on the occult and paranormal about to start. It's a small class, very competitive, but you don't need to worry about that."

I made a show of thinking it over. I'd been plenty reluctant to join his little following the last time I'd been there, and I didn't want to seem too eager. I'm no expert investigator, but it seemed to me that I should be as consistent as possible, while telling him as little as possible. "When and where?" I finally asked.

He leaned back on the couch and spread his hands to indicate the living room. "Right here, at five o'clock on Thursday," he said.

I nodded again. "Do I need to bring anything?"

"A notebook and pencil would be fine, but that's it. We'll work out course materials as we go; there isn't really a textbook for this kind of thing. At least not until we write it." He laughed.

I stood up to go, and he followed suit. He stuck out his hand. "I'm really glad you came back, Jed," he said. "We're going to learn so very much from each other this semester. Have you got a place to stay?"

"Yeah," I replied. "I'm good. I'll see you Thursday." I headed for the door, unsure if this was a good thing or not.

He saw me out, smiling widely the entire time. He didn't seem sinister at all; he came across more like a kid at Christmas. I was inclined to think he couldn't have been the one who sent the homunculus after me, until I remembered what he might consider Christmas. I remembered some of the volumes in his library, probably in the basement of the old house by now. They weren't uplifting, let's put it that way. Some of the volumes he had in his possession I'd been uncomfortable even opening, and that was when I was just sort of stumbling around in the dark.

I headed back toward the center of campus to meet up with Dan. One way or another, this was going to get interesting.

It seemed to take forever for Thursday to come along. Not so much because I was looking forward to the class starting; I spent the next two days keyed up and tense, watching and listening for any sign of the homunculus coming back for us.

Sitting and waiting has never been all that enjoyable to me, even when I was a Marine, where about ninety percent of your time is spent doing just that. The placid, affluent surroundings of the college seemed to make the threat that much more oppressive.

Finally, I was walking up onto the porch again. The sun was still up, and the trees hadn't started turning color yet. It felt like it should be dark, with a cold wind stirring naked tree branches and fallen leaves, but that was just my own trepidation talking.

There were four younger people waiting in the living room when I walked in. It was a warm evening, so the fireplace was cold. The chairs and couches had been rearranged so there was an open space next to the fireplace, with a whiteboard set up on an easel. I found a chair near the door and sat down, observing the rest of the class.

Three of them were gathered on the couch. They'd glanced up at me when I walked in, then went back to their conversation. Two were girls, wearing the near-uniform of skinny jeans and close-fitting t-shirts. The guy wasn't dressed much differently. I kept my lip from curling as I looked him over. Styled hair, earring, a pink t-shirt on a body mostly bereft of muscle, skinny jeans, canvas shoes…he was the image of the effeminate college kid that I'd learned to detest while a Marine. I still consider it a quite rational dislike.

The fourth was an older guy, not quite my age, but mid to late twenties at least. He was sitting by himself, dressed fairly conservatively, with a small, black notebook in his hands that he was thumbing through. He didn't even look up as I entered the room.

I checked my watch. I was about fifteen minutes early, yet another habit I'd never kicked from the Marine Corps. Several more students filtered in as I waited. They were a pretty even mix of young men and women, generally tilting toward the tattoos, dyed hair and piercings set, though the last four were all pretty normal-looking. By the time Ashton came into the room, there were about sixteen of us waiting. It made the living room a little cramped.

Ashton was still dressed exactly the same way he had been when I'd met with him a couple of days before. His hair was just as flyaway and slightly disheveled, but there was an eager gleam in his eyes, one that raised my hackles a bit. He had a stack of very old, leather-bound books and a cloth-wrapped lump in his arms. That lump made me even more uncomfortable. What was he planning on kicking this class off with?

He put the books down on the coffee table in the center of the room, then placed the cloth-wrapped bundle beside them. He looked around at the class with a smile. "Well, it looks like everyone's here, so let's get started, shall we?

"Welcome to 'The Occult: A New Examination.' This class is going to be a little different from your average folklore class. We're not going to be examining these things from a condescending, 'we know everything' sort of viewpoint. We will be examining old knowledge and exploring the hidden world, if it exists. So, before we begin, you need to let go of your cynicism and skepticism, and approach this subject with an open mind. Are some of the stories and legends out there nothing but myth and superstition? Of course. But is it also possible that some of them, dismissed by modern, mechanized society, are actually grounded in truth? That's what we're going to find out in the next few months.

"Is there, in fact, another world existing parallel to our own, one inhabited by beings other than us? Is there a way to communicate with these beings, be they spirits or some other sort of inhuman creatures? I think there might be, and over the course of this class, we will be examining the ways people have attempted to reach this other world throughout history. We might even take a few steps down the rabbit hole ourselves before the course is over." He smiled. He was really excited about this.

He paced back and forth in front of the darkened fireplace. There were enough people in the living room that he had a grand total of about five feet to pace, but he was brimming with nervous energy, so he paced. "Over the last century, the occult has been in and out of vogue in Western society. For the most part, however, it has always been in the shadows, its practitioners viewed with disapproval, fear, and hatred. The authorities of ancient Rome condemned sorcery, painting it as a terrible force of destruction and evil. The Church persecuted practitioners and inquirers into the occult mercilessly. Now, in our day and age, while those who are curious about the unseen and unknown are no longer subject to the Iron Maiden or burning at the stake, they are mocked and derided as delusional by a secular society.

"All of the above examples dismissed the occult as nothing but superstition. But I say that it is the fear of knowledge that makes for true superstition. The occult challenges us to look beyond the mundane world. It can be frightening, but then, what exploration of the unknown is not? I believe that by studying these more mystical aspects of the world, we might well discover truths and knowledge that could change all our lives."

He picked up the topmost book that he'd set down on the coffee table. "This is an original copy of *The Codex of the World of Spirits*. It took me a long time to track this volume down. Most experts in the field don't even believe it exists. According to word passed down by those who actually believe in its existence, it has been ruthlessly suppressed for centuries." His brief smile was almost a smirk. "You probably don't want to know what I had to pay to get my hands on this, but I can assure you that it didn't come out of your tuition." The rest of the students joined in his chuckle.

I glanced around, taking the measure of my "fellow" students. For the most part, all I saw was eagerness. There wasn't any visible discomfort from Ashton's words. I had been pretty sure that he'd hand-picked the students from his little following already, and the reactions I was seeing seemed to confirm that. The only real exception was the guy with the black notebook, who simply watched impassively and scribbled notes.

"This is the reason why there isn't a textbook for this class," Ashton explained, hefting the worn volume, and motioning to the other books on the table. "These are the textbooks, and there aren't many copies of any of them in existence. Furthermore, well...we aren't going to be following all that much of a structured 'class' here. We're going to be exploring and learning about these things, whether or not they exist, and how they interrelate with the 'real world' as we're used to it. You could say we'll be writing the textbook here."

He proceeded to go into some of the provenance of each of the obscure grimoires he had dredged up to base the class on. I won't repeat most of it. Some of them still exist. That lump was still shrouded in its towel, sitting on the coffee table next to the books. I looked at it, trying to see what it might be. For some reason, as Ashton's explanations semi-faded into the background, that thing started to grab my attention.

Its shape wasn't readily ascertainable. It looked like it was about eight or nine inches tall, and taller than it was wide. There was something about it that bothered me, but I couldn't put my finger on it. I felt sure that Dan could have picked it out in a heartbeat, but he was better placed as backup. I was the one who had made first contact with Ashton, and I was the one he'd been willing to invite into his inner circle. So I had to make do. I glanced at my watch, already anxious to get out and go over what had happened with Dan.

Ashton opened the class up for questions. The kid in the pink shirt and skinny jeans raised his hand. "Professor," he said, sounding as whiny and effeminate as I'd expected him to, "can you tell us where you did find some of these books? I like to think I've made a pretty extensive study of these sorts of works, and I haven't heard of most of them."

Ashton smiled. "Several of them I came across buried in the campus library, believe it or not," he said. "A lot of these sorts of books have found their way into libraries essentially without the librarians' notice or knowledge. They've gotten sold in estate sales when certain occult collectors die, or some of them simply seem to drift into people's hands without any way of finding out how. Some of it is quite mysterious, and while I'd like to find out how it happens, that's not really part of this class; we've got too much else to explore. Maybe it could be a subject for some later inquiry, though."

I kept my expression carefully neutral. Maybe I was the only one in the room who found the idea of occult objects appearing in people's possession without apparent cause sinister, but it didn't sound like a good thing. I happened to glance over at the other guy with the black notebook, and noticed him writing in it, his eyes focused on the page, frowning. When he glanced up, the look in his eyes wasn't that of a fascinated, eager college student. It was cold, calculating, and hard.

He must have felt me watching him, because he glanced over just as I looked back at Ashton. He studied me for a second, then went back to his notebook.

Most of the rest of the questions were fairly banal. I found myself tuning them out and turning my attention back to that cloth-wrapped object. I realized that Ashton had brought it up, but hadn't exposed it at all, or even mentioned it. Why not? What was it?

The more I studied it, the more sinister it seemed to become. The rest of the sound and light in the room seemed to fade. I could almost have sworn that the thing moved under the cloth.

Then Ashton started wrapping things up, and snapped my attention back to the rest of the room. "I don't want to get too in-depth tonight," he said, "this little meeting was just to get acquainted and give you an idea as to what we're going to be doing in this class. It's going to be intense, I'll tell you that. I want to give you all a day or so to think about what you're going to be getting into here. Give it some thought, and see if you're ready to have your entire world changed. If you are, I'll see you back here tomorrow evening."

There was a general bustle as everyone got up. The effeminate kid and his two female companions were chattering amongst themselves as they went out. Most of the rest were fairly subdued. The dude with the black notebook studied me, blank-faced, as I got up to leave.

"Jed, could you wait a second?" I turned from the door to see Ashton looking at me, his hand on that cloth-wrapped lump.

Chapter 5

I stepped away from the door. The blank-faced guy walked past me, glancing at me as he went. There was something about that guy, something that didn't fit with the rest of Ashton's supernatural groupies. I wanted to talk to him, to try to figure out what he was doing there, but Ashton was the guy I was sure I was there for, so I stayed. The guy with the black notebook went out the door, and disappeared around the hedge quickly.

Now I was left in the room with Ashton, alone. Alone with him and that cloth-covered lump that I really didn't want to get any closer to.

"So, what do you think?" Ashton asked as the door closed behind me. "I know it was kind of a tease, but some of these kids aren't as well-versed as you or I. They're eager to learn, but they have no experience with the real spooky side of life yet. I wanted to ease them into it."

So I was going to be his confidant on this little venture into the weird? I can't say I liked that idea, but getting closer would make my investigation easier.

Under his shining, excited gaze, I realized I needed to say something in response. "No, that's probably a good idea," I managed. "It's probably better to slowly get used to the idea than to have something freaky come out of the night all of a sudden."

He sobered somewhat, though his enthusiasm was still brimming over. He was really, really excited about this class. "Yes, that's right; your first exposure *was* fairly traumatic. Which is, of course, why I'm taking this track with the class. But I wanted to show this to you before I showed any of the others." He was like a kid on Christmas morning as he pulled the cloth off the lump.

It was a short, asymmetrical stone or clay tablet. Whether it had been deliberately shaped that way, or broken at some point, I couldn't really tell, but as I studied the symbols etched into it, I became pretty certain that it had been that shape when they were carved.

They weren't any occult symbols I recognized, but then, I hadn't made much of a study of such things yet, and I was pretty sure that Dan would warn against getting too deep into such a study if I did. Of course, they weren't really *any* symbols I recognized, either. The only thing I did recognize was the sense of unease I got when I looked at them. A couple made my stomach twist a little if I focused on them more than a second or so.

"What is it?" I asked.

Ashton looked like he was about to start bouncing. "It's one of the Kozheozersky Tablets." He looked at me like that was supposed to mean something. I raised my eyebrows and shrugged.

He sighed, frustrated. Apparently, my experience in the desert and subsequent search for answers was supposed to have educated me more extensively on such artifacts. "Kozheozersky is a monastery in northwestern Russia. According to legend, there were six Tablets, containing occult knowledge, written in code, that the monks held in secret in a vault below the monastery. It is one of the most isolated monasteries in the world; no roads lead to it. But someone managed to steal four of the Tablets during the Bolshevik Revolution. No one knows for sure where all of the others are, though most authorities I talked to believe that at least one still sits in the monastery's vault. But this one showed up in an estate sale in Maine two years ago. That's where I found it."

I eyed the thing a little skeptically. It wasn't that I doubted that the thing was somehow connected with the occult; it seemed almost alive, projecting a sort of palpable malevolence. It was just that I wasn't sure about the whole "ancient, mysterious tablet bit." I hadn't encountered anything like that so far. "So, if it's written in code, how does anybody find the key?" I asked, not sure I wanted to know the answer.

He leaned forward conspiratorially, his hand still on the tablet, and an almost fanatical fire in his eyes. "That's the beauty of it," he said, his voice dropping to just above a whisper. "You don't unlock the secrets of the tablet. The tablet reveals the secrets to you."

I confess I must have looked at him like he was losing his mind. He chuckled nervously, as if realizing how crazy that sounded. He straightened and seemed to gather himself a little. "I know, it sounds crazy, but there have been times where I could understand the symbols. They don't change, but the meanings do." He looked down at the tablet with a look of awe and reverence. "It's the strangest thing. It doesn't always happen, but about four times, I've studied the symbols, and realized there was a message there. Once I'd copied it down, they didn't seem to mean anything anymore. But the things it's told me…" His voice trailed off as he continued to stare at it. I wasn't entirely sure that he realized I was there anymore.

If I'd thought the tablet seemed malevolent before, now it was far, far worse. The fact that Ashton didn't see anything sinister in these inexplicable revelations didn't bode well for his sanity or his discernment. I wondered if that thing wasn't what had gotten him on this path in the first place. I mentally added the tablet to my list of "things to smash." Those books were already on it, and I didn't even know for sure what all they contained yet.

I started toward the door, somehow reluctant to turn my back on the tablet. While it was just an inanimate lump of stone or clay, it seemed like it was somehow aware of me, and it was not happy that I was there. Ashton didn't seem to notice my movement away, until I was at the door and opening it.

Then, his eyes still fixed on the tablet, he said, "See you tomorrow, Jed." His voice was low, flat…dead. I had the sudden horrible thought that it wasn't him speaking.

I got the hell out of there.

Dan picked me up on the curb. He'd been just down the block the entire time. His face was tight as he pulled away. "How'd it go?" he asked.

"Oh, he's dabbling, all right," I said. "Possibly worse than dabbling. You ever hear of the Kozheozersky Tablets?"

He glanced at me, his eyes a little wide. "He's got one?"

"He sure thinks he does," I said. "And even if it's not, whatever that thing is, there's something very wrong about it. I could feel it." I didn't know how to explain it beyond that, but Dan just nodded as if I didn't have to.

"What else?"

I gave him the short rundown, including the books, the planned curriculum, and, almost as an afterthought, I described the guy with the black notebook. "He didn't seem to fit in there like the rest of the groupies," I said.

Dan squinted thoughtfully at the street. "Interesting. Keep an eye on him. He might just be a journalist, or just a curious skeptic. Could even be a debunker. Or…he could be someone involved, on one side or another."

We were getting off campus now, and I was starting to relax a little. Only then did I realize just how wound up I'd been in that house. I hadn't been that tense since Al Anbar, and that included the times I'd been in some very dark places poking around the occult.

"You think he might be on our side, but somehow not a part of the Order?" I asked.

He nodded. "There are a few. Not many, and they tend to be a paranoid bunch. Some of them have clashed with the Order over the years, usually believing us to be a bunch of devil worshipping Papist sorcerers." He chuckled at my look of incredulity. "There are those people out there. Just look up conspiracy theories about the Jesuits some time. Some people don't even need to know about the Otherworld or the occult to believe that somehow the Catholic Church is in league with the Devil."

I absorbed that as we headed for the campsite where we'd set up. The sun was starting to go down, and the light was turning yellow. The leaves were just starting to turn, in the smaller groups of birches and aspens among the evergreens.

"You think that the tablet is what's causing the trouble?" I asked.

It took him a minute to reply. "Maybe, but it sounds like there are plenty of possibilities. If it really is one of the Kozheozersky Tablets, it could definitely be associated with some kind of malign influence. Bear in mind, though, that, folklore to the contrary, no inanimate object can have any sort of influence in and of itself. It can't be possessed, but it can be used by something else as a sort of red herring. If something is communicating with him through it, or appearing to do so, it's because he's already opened himself up to that influence." He sighed. "The thing you've got to understand is that while there are plenty of real monsters and demons in the shadows, most of the time they can't have any influence without people allowing it. You start concentrating on artifacts, and you miss the most important factor. Remember, it's ultimately a spiritual war that occasionally spills into the physical."

"So you're saying that he got himself into it by looking too deep?" I asked.

"Essentially, yes. It sounds harsh, but sooner or later you've got to make a choice. Whatever has happened to cloud some of these people's minds, they still at some point made the choice to go into these things, to listen to the whispers in the dark."

There was another long silence, as I thought that over, mentally adding in my own time treading into places and looking into things that I probably would have been better off avoiding. "Dan," I ventured slowly, "I've got to admit, after finding out how close I came to getting myself in too deep...well...this is a little uncomfortable to be delving this deep again. It just seems like I just figured out how close I got to getting burned, and now I'm going bonfire-jumping."

He didn't answer until we'd pulled into the campsite and found our spot. Only once we'd pulled in and he'd stopped the engine did he speak.

"You're a vet, Jed. You know about duty, and about risk. All I can really say at this point is that it's necessary. It's dangerous, but it's necessary. It's a calling. As long as you're careful, you'll have the grace necessary to keep your focus where it needs to be." He looked at me seriously. "Make no mistake, though, you have to be constantly vigilant. A Hunter I used to know wasn't." He wasn't looking at me anymore. "He's gone. Lost in more ways than one. He got too close and, well…he went over."

He didn't say anything more. He didn't have to. Just those words were chilling enough.

We got out and set about making supper. Well, I made supper. Dan prowled the edge of the campsite, looking for any sign of the homunculus or anything else that might come after us. There was nothing, and we ate in moody silence. I was still thinking about just what I'd gotten myself into, or *back* into. I'm sure Dan was thinking about the turncoat Hunter he'd told me about.

When we finally turned in, neither of us slept very well.

Chapter 6

In spite of the severe sense of foreboding I got that first night, the next two weeks went relatively quietly. Class came and went, and it was mostly note-taking and exploration of what little was known about ancient sorcery. There was surprisingly little. In spite of the promise of arcane knowledge encased in those leather-bound volumes on the coffee table the first night, most of them were histories of rituals, magical practices, and ancient secret societies, most of them apocryphal. Class on the third day of the second week was actually interrupted when the guy with the black notebook noticed an anachronism in one of the "contemporary" accounts of Sumerian rituals that dated the book to the mid-nineteenth century.

Ashton wasn't happy about that. The fact was, as I compared notes with Dan after class each day, most of what was getting peddled as ancient knowledge in these books was actually fantasy made up in the late 1800s and early 1900s.

"We found a 'grimoire' back about five, six years ago," Dan told me. "This was at the center of a really, really nasty case. There was a cult up in the West Virginia hills; these guys were like something out of *The Hills Have Eyes*, just without the mutation crap. Weird, secretive bunch, with a history of assault, battery, and robbery. They murdered a couple of kids; sacrificed 'em. Because of all the weird, Satanic crap the group was into, the local sheriff talked to the parish priest, who called us in.

"It was ugly. The whole place turned into a bloodbath when the sheriff's department went in. Six deputies shot, and every one of the cult dead. We didn't find any Otherworlders or anything like that, and when we finally found their 'Book of the Power,' it was an old gothic novel from a failed writer in 1901."

He'd shaken his head as he stirred the fire. "Sometimes evil doesn't need to intervene directly. People will tend toward it without any help from the Abyss at all."

I didn't think any of the books Ashton was using as direct sources were quite that off, but at the very least they were inventions to lend authenticity to whatever society was trying to create a mythology for itself. Most of them were a mix of Freemasonry and Ariosophy, the manufactured occult basis for "Aryan" society that formed some of the mythology of Nazi Germany. I wasn't sure how familiar Ashton was with that angle; I'd had no idea until Dan filled me in one night at the fire.

I was finding out just how much of the "occult" really was just smoke and mirrors, along with just how dangerous even that could be. The inhabitants of the Abyss could make inroads using the smoke and mirrors just as easily as they could with the real stuff.

The easy part ended after the second week.

The living room was darkened, with only a couple of lamps lit as we filed in. The evenings were getting noticeably darker, and the leaves were starting to fall from the trees outside. There was enough of a chill in the air that evening that there was a fire crackling in the fireplace.

I found my usual seat near the wall. The guy with the black notebook, who had eventually introduced himself simply as Ari, sat next to me. We nodded to each other; he was still wary, but it seemed like he'd developed a grudging acceptance toward me. I hadn't been the kind of eager beaver that Ashton had necessarily been hoping for; and Ari had noticed that. He was still suspicious, but he seemed like the type who was always suspicious of everyone.

Of course, my skepticism of some of the books in the class had not only deflated some of Ashton's enthusiasm, but it had alienated me from some of the students as well, particularly the trio who had been the first ones there on the first day. That made it easier to form a grudging bond with Ari, though it didn't appear to be helping me uncover whether or not it was Ashton behind the homunculus, or someone else using him as a blind.

Another thing I'd learned from Dan during those long conversations by the fire was that the enemy never came at you head on in this business. They always came at you sideways, disguising their intentions and means until they were inside your head, pulling at your weaknesses like puppet strings. It was entirely possible that Ashton was the guy we were supposed to be looking at, while someone else did the stuff in the dark.

Everyone was in the living room before Ashton showed up. Except for that first day, he'd usually been there waiting for us, but today he didn't come in until ten minutes after class was supposed to start.

He was noticeably upbeat. He'd finished the last couple of classes looking a bit like a kicked puppy, especially after discovering that the *Book of Ishtar* was actually written by an 1850s Masonic Lodge Grand Master. But today he looked like he'd found a new lease on life.

He sat down in his own chair, a carved, embroidered, Victorian affair, and rubbed his hands together. "Well, my friends," he began, "I know the last couple of avenues of study we've pursued have been a bit disappointing. I apologize for that, but as I said in the beginning, this class is about discovering new things, not just learning a bunch of facts to regurgitate on papers and tests." It was a neat way of dodging the fact that he hadn't done his homework sufficiently in class prep. "But I think we've finally got an experiment that should make up for the last couple of disappointments."

Now, after the last couple of "disappointments," anyone would be a little skeptical of his latest and greatest. Frankly, by this time I was really starting to doubt that Ashton was the bad guy Dan and I were looking for. The failures on the two texts suggested he really didn't know what he was doing. How could somebody fumbling around like he appeared to be doing manage to create and control a homunculus?

"I'm going to keep class short and sweet tonight, and not just because it's Friday. I don't want to give too much away, and there's too much preparation I have to do before this little experiment happens, so I'll just tell you to meet me at Powell Hill at three o'clock tomorrow morning." He grinned, his eyes twinkling with that kid-in-a-candy-store look he'd had at the beginning of the class. "I can assure you, this will be better than the last couple of books. By far." He held up his hands to forestall any questions from the Three Amigos, the little mental moniker I'd come up with for the effeminate dude, named Trevor, and his two sidekicks, Cathy and Amanda. "Just trust me." He was practically bouncing in his seat. "This will be good. You don't need to bring anything; in fact, just come with the clothes on your backs. No cameras. They might spoil things."

This did sound serious; but I withheld my judgment for the moment. This could prove to be as much of a dud as the books had.

Of course, as Dan had pointed out, the risk still existed that Ashton was going to end up going into the Abyss because of this stuff anyway, but that wasn't our job. We couldn't save everybody, but we could do what we could to keep the demons and monsters where they belong, instead of running around in the physical world.

"That's all for right now; you guys get a little time off this evening. Just be sure to be there in the morning." He was grinning from ear to ear; he really thought he had something.

For his sake, I hoped he was wrong again.

It was about two in the morning when I got to Powell Hill. I was wearing a jacket over my holstered Colt and about four spare magazines. A steel hip flask of holy water was in my back pocket, and the little silver crucifix that Father O'Neal had given me was around my neck. I would have taken my newly-acquired .45-70, but showing up to Ashton's little experiment with a long gun probably wasn't going to go over well. I still wanted to keep the reason for my interest quiet. This investigation was only going to have a hope of success as long as he kept talking to me.

I didn't have a light. I've avoided carrying a flashlight in the woods for a very long time. Given enough time to adapt, your eyes can see plenty in the dark. At least mine can. And shining a light around has the effect of letting everyone know that you're there, especially those who *aren't* shining lights.

I moved carefully through the trees. Powell Hill was in a park area of the campus, and it was a big park. I was far enough up the hill that I couldn't even see any of the lights from the campus proper. The trees were tall and thick; people rarely went all the way up the hill, though there was a trail. I wasn't sure why the hill was generally avoided, either. There weren't even any stories about it, at least not that I'd heard in the last couple of weeks. It just wasn't frequented.

Maybe this job was making me paranoid, but something about that struck me as significant. Usually, a hill in the woods that's this central to a college campus has *some* sort of traffic, usually for a view. There was a trail, and a clearing up at the top, but nobody seemed to ever go there. There weren't even any scary stories about it. It was just there, and nobody had any interest in it.

I hadn't been rushing, instead carefully placing my steps as I moved over the carpet of needles and fallen leaves, but as I neared the top I slowed down even more, concentrating hard on being quiet. Dan had warned me that if there were Otherworlders on the hill, just being quiet wasn't going to keep them from noticing me, but it could keep any human interlopers from knowing I was there. I'm good in the woods; always have been. I can move like a ghost at night. Granted, I mused, that might not be the best-chosen simile to use under the circumstances.

I hung back in the shadows of the trees, watching the clearing. Ashton was already there, rummaging in a backpack with a flashlight. He already had a large, leather-bound book and a bunch of various bits of junk scattered on the leaf-strewn grass in front of him.

I carefully scanned the treeline around the top of the hill. There was a rock outcropping at the top, and the northern treeline came right up to it; the clearing extended a little distance down the south side of the hill. It was still small enough that the trees screened any light from the campus or the town beyond.

In the dim light cast by the stars and Ashton's flickering flashlight, I saw that several of the trees had been blazed, the bark cut away in patches about the size of my head. The blazes were spaced about twenty feet apart, and it looked like they went all the way around the clearing. I suspected they were a part of Ashton's preparations.

After a brief search, always being careful not to fully expose myself to the clearing and Ashton's light, I found the nearest blaze. Sure enough, the bark had been hastily chopped away, down to the wood, and a symbol had been carved into the trunk of the tree.

I couldn't see it very well; details become difficult at night, even if your night-eyes are as good as mine. But I ran my hand over it, figuring out the shape as I went.

I can't describe it. If I could, I wouldn't. There was something distinctly *wrong* about it. The more I could picture it, the worse it got. I started to feel a little bit queasy.

That told me all I needed to know. Whatever Ashton had figured out, this had to be the real deal. Which meant that if I could, I had to do something to disrupt it, preferably before he could really get started.

At first I wasn't sure just how to go about that. I thought of using my knife to deface the symbols, but that was going to take time and probably make noise. It took me a minute to think of the flask in my back pocket.

Dan had suggested using the steel hip flask. It was sturdier than most containers people use for holy water. I pulled it out, unscrewed the cap, shook a healthy droplet on my finger, and splashed it in the Sign of the Cross on the symbol, silently pronouncing the Three Names as I did so.

There was actually a faint hiss, and I could have sworn I saw some smoke curl up from the tree trunk. When I touched the symbol again, it was just lines carved in the wood. I let out a breath I hadn't realized I'd been holding, and checked my watch, carefully shielding the glow from the clearing. I had about forty minutes before people were supposed to start showing up. I'd have to work quickly.

Slipping from tree to tree, staying in the shadows, I moved as quickly as I could without breaking branches or crunching leaves. I doused one symbol after another. After that first one, I didn't try to make out the shapes anymore. I found the blazes and splashed them with holy water, then moved on.

As I went, I started to feel like I wasn't alone in the woods., and it wasn't Ashton's presence that was bothering me. He was busy, muttering to himself as he tried to make sure he had everything laid out perfectly, consulting the old, leather-bound book he had open on the rock outcropping. No, this was something else. It was a sense of being directly observed, kind of like when you can feel someone staring at you. And there was a distinct feeling that whatever was watching me wasn't friendly.

Dan was out in those woods as well, with his .50 Beowulf, but I knew it wasn't him. For one thing, I knew where he was supposed to be, and he shouldn't have been close enough to be watching me. I stopped after the fifth symbol, and just looked and listened, straining my eyes to see if there was anything out there, and my ears to hear anything moving around. There was nothing but darkness and night noises. Whatever it was, if there was even anything there, it was being careful.

I almost thought I caught a whiff of something; a sour sort of smell, like the homunculus had left at Ray's place, but then it was gone.

I got the last symbol and faded back into the trees just as Ari showed up. I watched for a moment, wondering why he was the first one to arrive. Judging by his behavior during the rest of the class, I'd expected him to be one of the last ones to show.

He came up the trail and stopped just inside the clearing, taking a long look around. I could just make out his face in the nimbus of light from Ashton's flashlight. It was as expressionless as always. He watched Ashton for a while, making no move to get closer than he already was.

There was the flickering glow of a flashlight down the trail. That was when I realized Ari had walked up here without one, just like I had. Why? The more I watched him, the more questions I had.

The students' arrival reminded me that I needed to head back down the hill and come the rest of the way up the trail. Appearing out of the woods to one side would raise questions, and I didn't want to have to try to answer them.

So I circled around the side of the hill, coming back out onto the trail when I couldn't see any lights on it. As luck would have it, by the time I'd come out onto the clearing, everyone else had already arrived.

Ashton was holding court at the rock outcropping. He had a brace of candles lit on it, and had traced several more symbols on the rock. A chalk circle with even more symbols had been drawn on the ground in front of the outcropping, and there were several objects, mostly mundane things like candlesticks, knives, and a couple of animal bones, placed carefully among the symbols.

Even more ominously, the Kozheozersky tablet was sitting on the rock behind Ashton, who had donned what I imagined was supposed to be a robe, but looked more like a smoking jacket. At least he hadn't tried to put on some ridiculous headdress. I don't know if I could have kept a straight face if he had, the dread of the situation notwithstanding.

"My friends," he began, "I'm so glad you could come." As if anyone wouldn't have, given the way he had set this up. Everybody was committed anyway, by virtue of sticking with the class.

"I can't say that this is a ritual that hasn't been performed in a thousand years, or whatever, because there's no way to know that," he continued. "The knowledge has been out there for a long time, and there are several credible accounts of its having been successful. It is from this book"—he motioned to the leather-bound volume sitting open on the rock—"the *Codex of the World of Spirits*, which, I might add, is one of our sources that hasn't been shown so far to be a nineteenth century hoax." He laughed nervously.

The longer I watched him, and listened to him, the more I suspected that not only wasn't he sure that the ritual was going to actually work, he wasn't sure he *wanted* it to. He was scared.

"You're all familiar with séances, trying to call up the spirits of the dead. Well, this is something similar, but trickier. We're not going to be trying to contact a ghost; we're going to see if we can contact something much older."

He motioned to the clearing. "While I can't say with any certainty that this particular place has seen rituals like this before, I think it is likely. It matches the criteria the book puts forth for contacting a chthonic spirit."

I wasn't all that spun up on such things at the time, but even then I knew that that didn't sound good. I really, really hoped that blessing those symbols on the trees was enough to sabotage this little "experiment."

I hadn't noticed the cage at Ashton's feet earlier, but a rattle drew my attention as Ashton stepped away from it. "Most records of chthonic cults describe blood sacrifices to attract or appease the spirit, and the description of this ritual in the *Codex* is no different. I know," he said, as a couple of the girls made uncomfortable noises, "I know. It's kind of difficult for us to accept in this day and age, but remember, these beings aren't products of this day and age, and they don't particularly care about it, either. If we're going to explore this other world, and *really* see that it exists and how it works, we're going to have to do some things that might make us uncomfortable."

With that said, he turned toward the rocks and the candles burning on them. He carefully stepped through the chalk circle on the ground, making sure he didn't disturb any of the symbols etched there, and stood in front of the symbols on the rock. There he began to read from the book.

For a while, there was no sound but the increasingly frantic scratching of the rabbit in the cage, and Ashton's droning recitation. I was trying to watch everywhere at once, waiting for something to happen.

When Ashton pulled the trembling rabbit out of the cage and slashed its throat, I had my hand as close to my Colt as possible, without being obvious about it. Frankly, by then I probably could have had it out and ready, and none of the students would have noticed. They were all watching Ashton, hardly daring to breathe. There were a couple of whimpers when he killed the rabbit, and several of the students were visibly trembling. I was pretty sure most of them were reacting that way to the animal being killed, rather than what Ashton was trying to do.

The blood pattered on the rocks, and Ashton continued to read, his voice rising as he reached the culmination of the ritual. The wind picked up a little, rustling the trees.

I snapped my head to one side as I could have sworn I heard something snarl in the treeline. But there was nothing there. I took my hand off my pistol before anyone else noticed, but everyone was still completely focused on Ashton and the circle.

71

By the time he finished the final words of the conjuration, Ashton was shouting, though the sound didn't seem like it traveled very far. There wasn't even an echo; it was like the trees swallowed the sound.

For a long moment, there was no sound at all. Everyone seemed to be holding their breath, waiting to see what would happen. There was a definite tension, a sort of oppressive feeling in the air, like the hot, heavy feeling just before a thunderstorm.

The silence stretched on. I started to feel like we were being watched by something in the trees. For some reason, even without being able to see anything, I could tell it was big. Big, and mean, and angry. Whatever it was, it wasn't happy about our being there, or what had just happened.

A branch snapped out in the woods. It was almost as loud as a gunshot, the *crack* echoing across the hillside in a way that Ashton's shouts had not. Whether the ritual had worked as intended or not, there had definitely been something uncanny going on during the recitation.

Ashton was looking around, appearing more than a little bewildered and scared. "Something's not right," he whispered. "Something should have happened by now." He frowned down at the book. "I don't know what I got wrong…"

My eyes were drawn by what looked like movement in the trees, but again, there was only blackness. Had one of the candles made a shadow shift as it flickered, or had there been something else? I still had that oppressive feeling, like when somebody's staring at the back of your head. I was sure that there was *something* out there, watching us. The sense of malevolence was palpable.

Some of the other students seemed to be getting it now. Ari was looking around, his eyes as wide as he could get them, straining for a look at something, anything. The others were less intent, but still looking around at the trees, sensing that something wasn't right, but not sure what.

Then the noises started.

At first there was a crashing sound, as if something was running full-tilt through a thicket, and didn't care about not being heard. I say *something*, because it sounded a lot bigger than any man. Granted, size doesn't matter that much in the woods at night; I once came across a raccoon in a dead tree that was

72

making enough noise that I'd thought it had to have been an elk. But this definitely sounded like something big.

Then there was a rustle of movement all around the clearing, like dozens of feet pattering on the needles and leaves. Whispering hissed across the clearing, loud but somehow unintelligible. That started a couple of students freaking out. Nobody screamed, but a couple of gasps and outright squeaks got out.

Ashton didn't seem to notice. This was not the effect he'd been expecting. He was feverishly reading over the book, looking for where he'd gone wrong. I was easing back into the shadows, starting to reach for my Colt with one hand and the crucifix with the other. I knew Dan was out there…and that was when I realized that that put him right in the middle of whatever was making the noises. I felt a momentary pang of fear for my friend and mentor.

What finally snapped Ashton out of it was the thin, inhuman screech that came out of the darkness around the hilltop. Someone who wasn't there might suggest that it was an owl, but I know better. Whatever that thing was, it was no animal. There were no words in that cry, but there was a hate and malice that knew no boundaries, a thirst for pain and chaos. It was enough to freeze the blood. *That* got Ashton's attention.

He forgot the book for a moment, looking up and around. The fact that there was nothing to see seemed to reassure him for a moment, and then that screech went up again. It sounded closer this time.

"Something's gone wrong," he said, still sounding distracted, and not seeming to be aware of the sheer terror gripping most of his students. I glanced over at Ari, who, somewhat to my lack of surprise, looked a little more poised and ready than scared. The rest were huddled together like a flock of sheep, staring out into the blackness of the woods.

The noises were getting more frantic. It sounded like several dozen people or creatures were out there, stamping around in the undergrowth and fallen branches. What might have been whispers and snarls were barely discernible in the sound of movement and cracking sticks. Then, just as suddenly as it had begun, it all went silent again.

Except for a whisper that sounded like it was right next to my ear. *I know it was you that thwarted me, Hunter,* the voice said, dripping with menace. I glanced around, but it didn't look like anyone else could hear it. *I will not walk the waking world tonight. These mewling animals will not taste my fury yet. But one day, I will step forth into your world, and when I do, I will find you in short order. And then, I will make your torment last and last, until finally, with what little is left of your ravaged body, you curse God, and then...oh, and then, then, you will die. And when that happens, your suffering will truly begin.*

It was a less detailed, but somehow more frightening, version of what the demon in the Drop Inn had said. But instead of elaborating, the thing fell silent, and after a moment, I could almost feel it turning away. The sense of something big and malevolent and powerful out in the woods faded, as though something had turned aside and slumped off into the night, leaving behind a promise of horror to come.

"Um," Ashton ventured, "I think perhaps we should go now. I don't know what went wrong, but something definitely did, and it might be dangerous to be out in these woods right now. I don't know what was making those noises, but to be on the safe side, we should go back down the hill as a group." He looked back toward the circle and his paraphernalia. "I'll come back for this stuff when it's light." That was probably the smartest thing he'd said all night.

I kept toward the back as the group started down the trail behind a cone of bright light from the flashlights. Ashton was toward the front, still obviously preoccupied. I was entirely uninterested in discussing what went wrong with his little ritual, though I suspected I'd have to face that conversation when we got back to campus. Until then, I kept my distance.

It was a rapid, noisy, stumbling descent. The trail was pretty rocky in places, and the rest of the students were concentrating more on watching the trees for some unknown horror to come out at them than they were on watching where they put their feet.

Nothing jumped out at us. Nothing made any more noises. But the group was still pretty shaken up even after we were back among the street lights on campus.

Ashton stopped at the porch. "I'd invite you all in, but I have to do some study and determine where the mistake happened. I think we can all agree, though, that *something* happened." He stared off into the dark, thinking hard. "I'll see you all tomorrow." He must have been rattled; it was Saturday. Nobody would be back until Monday night. Without another word, he turned and headed inside.

I was just as glad to avoid his buddy-buddy discussion of the issue. I didn't stick around. I headed for the agreed-upon corner where Dan would pick me up.

He was late.

I waited in the splash of light from the streetlight for a very tense ten minutes before he pulled up. In the old days, when people were the enemy, I'd have hidden in the shadows, but that night the shadows were the last place I wanted to be. I wasn't sure that I believed that thing when it said "another time."

"Sorry I'm late," Dan said, as I jumped in the cab and slammed the door. As soon as I was in, he was rolling again. "Things got a little dicey in the woods. Couldn't see anything, but there were some very angry creepy-crawlies out there in the dark. Had a few big branches tossed at me."

"So, now what?" I asked. "It's pretty obvious that he's in deep."

"He is," Dan agreed, "but we don't know for sure that he's behind the homunculus. Have you seen it?"

I shook my head. "No, I haven't." I sighed. "He hasn't mentioned anything about one, either. He's such a kid in a candy store about this stuff that I'd expect him to start gushing about it as soon as he got one to work." There was always the possibility that he was keeping some things to himself; he certainly tended to get excited about "surprises," but I couldn't be sure. I finally said as much.

Dan nodded. "We still have to find that homunculus and put it down, whether he's behind it or not. Either way, we're going to have to stick around and make sure he *can't* manage to unleash one of these things. From what happened up on that hill, whether or not he's behind the homunculus, he's dabbling in some very dangerous stuff." He frowned at the darkened road as we turned away from the campus and onto the road to the

75

campsite. "It'd be best if we can bring him around; it's always preferable to convince these people to change their ways than shut them down the hard way. Go to class on Monday, see what more you can find out; I'll go see the local padre and see if we can sit the good professor down for a chat."

Of course, it wasn't going to be that simple.

Chapter 7

On Monday I showed up to the house an hour before class was supposed to start. I'm not entirely sure why. I certainly wasn't eager to get drawn into Ashton's brainstorming session about what had gone awry with his ritual the night before. But I was restless sitting at the campsite waiting all day, so I had Dan drop me off early. The two days of the weekend had dragged on, filled with a sort of dread that I couldn't quite put my finger on, and that Monday afternoon it had just come to a head.

Fall was definitely moving along, especially at that altitude. The trees had turned orange, yellow, and red, and there was a definite cold, smoky smell in the air. But that wasn't the main thing I noticed when I stepped through the gate into the yard.

At first, I just knew something was off. It took me a minute to figure out what it was. I stood there, looking around and sniffing the air, and that's when I got it.

There was a faint sour smell in the air. It reminded me of the stale vomit smell the homunculus had had floating around it.

The house's windows were dark, curtains partially drawn. There was no sign of life or movement. I carefully looked around for any sign of the homunculus, but saw nothing, just the house and the trees, looking as normal as ever, but that smell had just made everything seem more sinister.

So, my assumption that Ashton would have been too excited to keep his mouth shut about getting a homunculus to work had been wrong. It seemed like he was better at keeping secrets than he appeared.

What did that mean for my mission? What did he know about me? Was his friendly act all a trap?

For a long minute, I just stood there, looking at the door. All I could think about was how much I didn't want to go into that house again. It felt too much like walking into a firesack, knowing that the bad guys are on the high ground, watching and waiting for you.

But I walked up the steps anyway.

I was committed and I knew it. Whatever happened, it was too late to back out. This thing was hunting me, or at least dogging my steps, whatever Ashton had to do with it. Running wasn't going to solve anything. Neither was trying to hide in a hole. If I was going to be free of this, free of the consequences of my incautious poking around, I had to confront it, and put this thing down. As much as I had questioned whether or not Ashton was really who I was looking for, that smell had told me that he was connected with the homunculus *somehow*.

I knocked on the door, peering through the glass, but the entryway was empty and dark. I thought I might have seen a little movement, but it was hard to tell. I told myself I was just jumpy after the previous night's activities on the hill, but if Ashton was in deep enough to animate a homunculus, who knows what could be prowling around the shadows in that house?

After a couple of minutes, I knocked again. The heebie-jeebies were getting stronger, and I was momentarily glad I'd decided to bring my Colt, concealed at the small of my back, concealed weapons laws be damned. I looked around the porch, but there was nothing to see but a few leaves stirring in the late afternoon breeze.

I was about to knock again, when the door opened. I hadn't even seen Ashton through the glass, suggesting how dark it was inside. "Oh, Jed," he said. "You're early; I wasn't expecting anyone for another hour."

"Sorry," I replied. "I didn't really have anything else to do, so I figured I'd show up a little early." I looked at my watch. "I guess I overdid it a little."

"No, it's all right," he said, opening the door wider. "Come on in. I was just studying, trying to figure out what went wrong last night." His expression was blank, and his voice was low and flat.

I followed him inside. This time he led me through the living room and into what had to be the study. The walls were floor-to-ceiling bookshelves. An old writing desk was in the center, piled with old books and notes, and there were a couple of deep chairs in the corners. The only light on in the room, apparently in the entire house, was a floor lamp next to the writing desk.

Ashton went to the desk. The *Codex* was open in the middle of the stacks of books and papers. "I went back a few hours after the sun came up to collect the paraphernalia that we left up on the hill this morning," he said. He didn't really look at me; he almost seemed to be only speaking to me by virtue of my being in the same room. His focus was entirely on the *Codex* and the tablet next to it. "I've gone over it and over it. I don't understand. I copied *every* symbol in the *Codex*'s description precisely. I was *certain* of the placement of the ceremonial objects. Everything was in place. It should have worked. We should have met"—he pronounced a name that he shouldn't have been able to twist his tongue around, and that started to give me a headache—"but nothing happened."

"Something happened," I pointed out. "It just wasn't what you were expecting. There was definitely a reaction out in the woods."

"Hmm." He still seemed distracted, absorbed in the artifacts in front of him. I was really starting to wonder what kind of effect they were having; even though Dan had assured me that the objects themselves could contain no particular power, he seemed almost hypnotized by them. "Yes, there was something, but it wasn't what was supposed to happen." He made the gargling, headache-inducing noise again, "...was supposed to manifest in the circle. That was the whole point of the ritual. If he didn't come, then I must have gotten something wrong...but I didn't. I carefully checked and double-checked. Everything was right."

He finally looked directly at me. "What do you think?" I resisted taking a step back. His eyes were bright, intense; almost feverish. "If I got everything right, something else must have happened, something that interfered with the ritual."

He was getting uncomfortably close to the truth. While a confrontation might settle things, I found I didn't really want this thing to come to a head here and now. I wasn't ready. Frankly, I was scared. The implications of that sour smell out front had thrown me a little. My assumptions of what I was dealing with with Ashton had been thrown out, and now I wasn't certain I could handle him if it came down to a fight. I knew for a fact that I wasn't prepared to face the homunculus.

But at the same time, I got the feeling that out-and-out lying didn't fit very well with my new profession. I'd have to be as evasive as possible. "I guess that makes sense," I said.

"You were the last one to get there, Jed," he said, still studying me with that uncomfortable intensity. "Did you see or hear anything on the way that might have given a clue as to what might have interfered?"

I shrugged, forcing myself to meet that feverish gaze. "I wouldn't even know for sure what to look for," I told him. "You know a lot more than I do about this sort of stuff."

He narrowed his eyes, searching my face, then turned back to the tablet, nodding slightly. "Yes, of course; I just thought maybe you'd studied enough since you left here to have picked up on some of the tell-tales, but then, you haven't been gone all that long, have you?" He whipped his head around to look at me again. The mercurial way his thoughts were apparently racing was starting to freak me out a little. The nerdy, excitable, curious professor was gone, replaced by this driven, distracted man. I wondered how much of this had been just below the surface all along. I was realizing that, putting aside the professorial, inquisitive façade, this was a very dangerous man.

"Why were you the last one there, Jed?" he asked. "That's not like you; you're usually very punctual, if not early, like today. What kept you?"

Crap. I obviously couldn't tell him I was out in the woods sabotaging his ritual; if he got angry and called the

80

homunculus I was dead. I was feeling cornered and unprepared, like I'd walked into the lion's den with my pants down. Mixed metaphors, I know, but it kind of fit at that point.

"I kind of wandered off the trail," I said. Technically, it was true, though there hadn't been a lot of "wandering" involved. "It took me a while to find it again." Just enough time to bless the outer glyph circle and poison it against whatever that thing under the hill was.

He stared at me sort of sideways, with a calculating look on his face, as if gauging whether or not he believed me. I forced myself not to hold my breath, but to meet his gaze mildly and keep my body relaxed. *Can I draw and shoot him before he calls that thing?* I wondered. I hoped I didn't have to find out.

Finally, his eyes wandered off, drifting across the room until they finally rested on the tablet again. I studied the thing, but saw nothing different. When I glanced back at Ashton, though, he seemed almost to be reading something. Another look to be sure, but there was no text, nothing beyond the vaguely disturbing symbols scribed into the tablet.

"There won't be class today," he told me, sounding distracted and distant again. "I have to study. We can't continue until I've figured out what went wrong. And until I've fixed it."

While he didn't look at me, and the tone of his voice never changed, I had the unmistakable feeling that the last sentence was a threat. I stepped away, never quite turning my back on him, ready to reach for my pistol if he suddenly decided to flip out.

But all he said was, "Tell the rest of the class if you see them, won't you?" He was still staring raptly at the tablet. The *Codex* appeared forgotten, now.

I got to the door and stepped through, only then daring to turn around. I immediately started checking every corner, almost sure that the homunculus was going to be waiting there with its blank eyes and idiot grin to grab me. I didn't have so much as a lighter on me, and I already knew what kind of good my .45 was going to do against it.

The house was dark as the sun headed for the horizon behind the trees. Ashton had most of the curtains drawn, so only a weak, orange glow lit the rooms, with deep, black shadows where it didn't reach. There weren't any west-facing windows in the living room, so there wasn't even that much illumination. The room was dark and gray, with even more pools of blackness where anything could be hiding. As I carefully moved between the furniture toward the front door, I kept thinking about how small the homunculus had appeared when it had attacked us at Ray's ranch, and how easily it could fit into some of those totally dark spaces.

I got to the door just as Ari and four more students mounted the porch and knocked. I opened the door, and Ari took a half step back, looking at me with a hint of surprise and suspicion in his eyes.

"Ashton's busy," I explained. "Really busy, which is why the lights are off. He said there's no class today, while he tries to figure out what went wrong last night."

There was a murmur among the rest of the students, which Ari didn't join in, instead studying me, and the darkened room behind me, intently. He could tell there was something off, but he didn't know for sure what. And I didn't think at that point that he was willing to ask me about it, either.

He wasn't. He just nodded, as taciturn as ever, turned, and went down the steps. He stopped at the gate to look back, studying me and the house one more time, before walking off down the leaf-strewn sidewalk.

I was the last one down the stairs, letting the others go ahead of me while I searched the shadows under the trees and around the hedge, looking for a glint of blank, black doll's eyes. Nothing appeared. Cautiously, I sniffed the air. There was still a hint of that sour stink, but it seemed a little bit less than when I'd first arrived. Or did it? I couldn't be sure, and I couldn't be sure how much of my perceptions were being influenced by the fact that I was scared stiff.

It took a few minutes to summon up the courage to step off that porch. I knew Dan was only about a block away, waiting in the truck, but if the homunculus was lying in wait for me in the shadows of the yard, a block away might as well be miles.

But nothing materialized as I went down the steps and across the yard, rubbernecking like mad for any movement or sign that something evil was coming to rip my head off. The evening breeze stirred a few leaves, and one of the old trees creaked, but I made it to the gate completely unmolested. It swung open without a sound and I was out on the street.

I tried not to rush as I walked toward where Dan had parked, only remembering when I was almost there that he wouldn't be there until later; he'd gone to the local Catholic parish to discuss the matter of Ashton's class with the local priest.

I tensed up even more, looking around at the mostly empty street. A few houses were showing lights, but there weren't many people actually living on that street; most of the houses were used as spillover space for the College, and it was getting late enough that most of the students and faculty that were still on campus were going to be in the main buildings, not up here in the auxiliaries.

I thought I heard something behind me, but a glance back showed it was just a gaggle of coeds a couple blocks down the street. Several of Ashton's students were still visible, walking away. I was momentarily somewhat reassured; there were other people nearby. But then I realized that I had no idea if the homunculus or its master would care if someone saw it turn me into a smear on the sidewalk. After all, what cop was going to believe that a man was murdered by a five-foot tall claymation figure?

I had just turned back toward where Dan usually parked, when a figure stepped out of the shadows of another hedge. I almost drew my pistol before I saw it was Ari.

"We need to have a talk," he said.

I stayed where I was. It vaguely felt like a shadowy version of a Western gunfighters' standoff. "About what?" I asked.

He took a step nearer. I'd relaxed a little, trying to appear somewhat non-threatening, but my hand was still on my belt, inches from my pistol. "About what's really going on in that house," he said. "About what happened on Powell Hill last night. About who you are, and why you're acting differently than the rest of these poor naïve idiots who are lapping up Ashton's occult poison."

"You're going to have to be a bit more specific," I temporized, trying to watch him while still looking around for the homunculus to come out of the dark.

It was too dark to make out much of his expression. "You're not a student. Ashton apparently knows you from somewhere. You're not a journalist—they don't usually reach for guns when somebody surprises them on the street. Are you a cop?"

Having already gotten quite paranoid enough for one night, I wasn't exactly on my best footing dealing with this. "Not exactly." The following pause was long enough that he must have decided that was all I was going to say.

"What exactly are you doing here, then?" he asked. "What's your interest in Ashton? You act like you know this stuff's dangerous, but here you are, up to your neck in it. Ashton treats you like his favored pupil, but you don't show anywhere near the enthusiasm of some of these kids. You're cautious, and you're always watching everything in the room like you're looking for a threat. I've seen that much. Who are you?"

"I might ask you the same question," I replied. "Why should I spill my guts to you? Who are you, and why are you asking me all this?"

He watched me for a second, as if thinking it over. Finally, he reached into his shirt, and pulled something out. It fell onto his chest. At first I couldn't see what it was, but then enough light hit it to glint off a silver crucifix. "Does this mean anything to you?" he asked.

I felt a rush of relief, and took my hand away from my pistol to pull my own crucifix out. "As a matter of fact, it does," I replied.

He let out what sounded like a half-sigh, half-laugh. He shook his head. "Well, I guess that explains that," he said. "What brings you here?"

"Correcting some old mistakes," I replied.

He turned somber. "I take it those mistakes involve Ashton?" he asked.

"To some degree," I replied. I sniffed the air. Yes, the sour smell was definitely still there, almost a block away from the house. "Do you smell that? Kind of like stale puke?"

He sniffed. "Barely. There's a hint there."

"That's a homunculus," I told him. "We're pretty sure Ashton's had it following me since I was last here a few months ago. It's killed several people already, and tried to kill us a few weeks ago."

Ari whistled softly. "Well, this just keeps getting better and better. I just came to investigate when Father Herschel heard that Ashton was teaching a very small, exclusive class on the occult. But between last night and what you just told me, it sounds like this is a lot more serious than I thought." He glanced at me sharply. "I take it you were the reason the ritual went wrong last night?"

I nodded. "Holy water on the outer ring of symbols."

"That'll do it." He looked around. "We should probably find someplace else to talk. If there's a homunculus around…I don't have anything to set it on fire. Do you?"

"Nope," I replied. "And that is making me a little nervous, let me tell you. We weren't even sure Ashton was actually connected to that thing until I smelled it just a little while ago."

"Come on, then," he said. "My car's over here." He led the way to a small Ford sedan. "You keep saying 'we,'" he said. "Who else is here with you?"

"A guy named Dan Weatherby," I replied. His eyebrows went up.

"Dan's here? That's good news. I worked with him a couple of years ago, down in New Mexico." He unlocked the car and I climbed into the passenger seat. "Where's your car?" he asked as he started the engine. "I've only ever seen you walk in."

"Don't have one at the moment," I admitted. "My truck's with Father O'Neal in Oregon. Dan's been dropping me off and picking me up. He should be at St. Mary's in town right now." I checked my watch to be sure. There was still at least an hour before class was supposed to have been finished.

Ari nodded as we pulled away from the curb. "Probably a good place to be right at the moment," he said. "Whatever Ashton was trying to summon last night might not have come through, but a lot of the local spooks got stirred up something fierce."

"Yeah, I noticed," I muttered.

"I've been doing this for five years," he said. "I've seen stuff like last night a few times now. It never gets any better; it still freaks me out." His hands tightened on the wheel. "I almost froze last night."

I didn't tell him, but right then, I saw a figure in the shadows beneath a big, gnarled oak a block from Ashton's house. It was short, and its head looked too big. "Well, we got out of it all right," I said. His confession made me a little bit uncomfortable; he'd been doing this for five years, and now I felt like the old hand. I'd been scared, sure, but I hadn't even gotten the shakes until we'd gotten well away from the weirdness up there on the hill.

It was a short drive to the church. Dan's Bronco was parked on the curb out front, and he was walking out of the front doors as we pulled up.

"Well, I'll be," he said, as we got out and he saw who was with me. "Ari Schwartz. Long time, no see." He walked over and shook Ari's hand. "What are you doing here?"

"I've been here," he said. "I've been sitting in on Ashton's special little occult class, along with your boy, here. I didn't know until about twenty minutes ago that he was one of us."

It was hard to see in the dim light of early evening, but there was a flicker of something across Dan's face, something vaguely stiff and cold, but it faded as quickly as it appeared, and he relaxed into a grin. "Well, it's always good to have some more backup." He looked over at me, and jerked his head toward the church. "We won't get any here, at least not for the moment."

I frowned. "The priest isn't going to help?"

He shook his head as he walked around to the door of his truck. "He's still wet behind the ears. One of the new, more worldly breed. He doesn't believe any of this stuff is real. He thinks it's all fantasy, and that there's nothing terribly wrong with any of it." My face must have registered my reaction, because he chuckled bleakly. "Yeah, there are some like that. It depends on what schools they went to. Just like politicians, some of the clergy don't want to think about the real evils that are out there. It's a lot easier to preach 'just be nice to people' than it is to face the fact that there are real evils, real demons out there, and that siding with them has real, eternal consequences. Father James is one of those who would rather take the easy route." He looked out my door at Ari. "You coming?"

Ari shook his head. "I'm going to turn in for a bit," he said. "I'll see you guys later." He headed back to his car. I watched him, frowning slightly.

"Okay, before we get into everything about the priest who doesn't believe in the Devil," I said, as I climbed into the passenger seat, "mind filling me in on that guy? He seems a little, well...*off.*" My initial relief at running into another Hunter here had worn off, replaced by disquietude at Ari's manner.

Dan frowned into the rear-view mirror, watching Ari get in his car and pull away. "Bit of a long story, actually," he said. "What did he tell you?"

"Just that he's a member of the Order, that he's been doing this for about five years, and that he knows you," I replied. "He said he worked with you in New Mexico."

Once Ari had pulled away and driven past, Dan put the truck in gear and started back toward the campsite. It took him a few minutes to say anything more.

"Ari Schwartz is a member of the Order," he said, "but he's never managed to be much of a Hunter. He's tried. Several times. He's never been able to stand his ground. The one time I worked with him, he wound up curled up in the fetal position, crying. And that was just against a single night-gaunt—scary to look at, and in league with much nastier things, but by itself not that dangerous."

He sighed. "While it's never a bad thing to have someone else nearby who knows the Otherworld and the supernatural, don't count on Ari Schwartz when things get spooky. I hate to say it, but if you do, you'll be disappointed, and it could get you and a bunch of other people hurt, killed, or worse."

That wasn't terribly reassuring, even though it kind of fit the picture that had begun to form when Ari had told me he'd almost "frozen" on the hilltop. "I guess that explains why he suddenly didn't want to stick around when we met up with you," I said. "He realized you remembered him, and didn't want to be here when his past came up."

"Don't get me wrong," Dan said. "He's not a bad guy. He tries. He's just not cut out for direct confrontation with the Otherworld. Or, really, with anyone else for that matter."

"Is he going to be a liability?" I asked.

"Potentially," he admitted. "I'd say treat him as just another student that you have to try to protect, but he'll try to be a Hunter when the time comes. Then you'll have to pull him out, after he gets himself in over his head. I can't promise I'll get there in time."

That was encouraging. "What about the priest?" I asked, changing the subject.

He shrugged. "It's more common than you might think. You've got to understand that most people never see this side of the world. Because they never see it, or they see only a tiny, fleeting bit of it, they explain it away. It's not an easy thing to process, that there really are monsters in the dark. It's entirely possible to believe in God, but not want to believe in the darker side, in the things that have willingly rebelled against Him. Priests can be just as susceptible to it as anyone."

"So we've got no support," I said, a sinking feeling settling in my stomach. "We're on our own."

"Not necessarily," Dan said. "I made a call before I left. A friend's on the way."

Class continued to be canceled for the rest of the week. The day before it was supposed to start again, we got a visitor at the campsite.

I heard the growl of his motorcycle as he entered the campsite and worked his way toward the back corner where our tent was pitched. I didn't know he was coming our way until he pulled up next to Dan's truck and killed the engine.

He was a rough-looking customer. Dressed head-to-toe in black motorcycle leathers, his face was lined, brown leather. When he took his sunglasses off, his eyes were as black as his garments and his hair. He wasn't wearing a helmet. His Fu Manchu mustache seemed to accentuate what looked like a semi-permanent scowl.

He lowered the kickstand and put his booted feet on the ground. He sat astride the bike for a moment, looking over the campsite, as he pulled his gloves off. I sat on a log by the tent, my .45-70 close at hand, and watched him back.

He looked like he should be a hitman for a drug cartel. The whole ensemble made the Roman collar at his throat look that much more incongruous.

"You must be the visitor that Dan's expecting," I said.

He turned those cold black eyes on me. "That would be me," he said, "unless he's waiting for more than one visitor." His voice was a low, gravelly growl. It fit the rest of his appearance.

I shook my head. "Just the one, or so he's told me." I stood up as he swung one leg over the bike and stood up. "I'm Jed."

"Father Ignacio Rojas," he replied, holding out a hand. "Where's Dan?"

"Right here," Dan said, coming out from behind the tent, where he'd been cutting firewood. He grinned, and Father Ignacio returned the expression, teeth flashing white beneath the Fu Manchu. "Good to see you, Father."

They shook hands, and Father Ignacio pulled up a log round next to the fire pit to sit down. "So," he said, "fill me in. Every detail."

Dan looked at me. I got down to it.

Father Ignacio was one of the Order's itinerant priests; they had no parish as such, but were free to wander the country and aid Hunters as they were needed. They were also all trained exorcists.

His scowl deepened as he listened, occasionally interrupting only to ask a pertinent question, then lapsing into attentive silence again. When I was finished, he continued to think for a moment. "Tough to say," he said. "There might be another hand puppet-mastering the situation. But the way you described his behavior the last time you spoke to him…" He shook his head. "There is some inimical influence at work. How much is his own doing, and how much is someone else getting to him in some way is hard to tell. We have to find out for sure. If we act too soon, and neutralize this Ashton without also neutralizing whatever or whoever is influencing him, we could only be setting the ground up for the next curious fool to get pulled in."

"How do we find that out?" I asked. "Or, maybe more precisely, how do we find out without going too deep?"

"Keep spying," Father Ignacio said bluntly. "A thousand years ago, we might have been able to be more open, but these days…" He shook his head. "We have to be quiet, and subtle. Besides, the enemy likes the shadows; they are creatures of lies and deceit, and they will run and hide if there's any stone left unturned for them to slither under."

He fixed me with that dark stare. "Just keep your head. Keep your eyes on what is right and good, and believe nothing the enemy tells you. Never forget that the Devil is a liar. He's *the* liar. Keep your eye on the ball, and you should come through all right." He smiled a little. "People often talk about God being on their side. Make sure you're on God's side. That's all I can really tell you."

I nodded. It was a small comfort.

I didn't know how much worse it was about to get.

Chapter 8

When I got there for class the next night, there was nothing set up in the living room. The fireplace was cold, and only one light was on. Most of the rest of the students were there already, with Ari keeping back in the shadows. He made eye contact once, and nodded.

After Dan's revelation, Ari's stone-faced coldness had taken on a new aspect. As I watched him, always taking care not to stare, I could see the signs of nervousness and fear, masked by the hard case act. He was petrified, but trying hard not to show it. He was desperately trying to be a Hunter. But I worried that Dan was right. He didn't belong here. He wasn't cut out for this.

I was contemplating how to break it to him, especially since I'd really just met him, when Ashton came into the room.

The sinister intensity and questing, unfocused hostility that had been there in that darkened study a week before were gone. The excited, shiny-eyed, inquisitive student was back. But now, having seen the other side, the darker side, I wondered how much of it was as much of an act as Ari's impassive toughness.

"Welcome back, everyone," he said. "Obviously, our previous experiment didn't work out. But, I think I might have found something that will not only make up for it, it will make what we were trying to do look like child's play."

I suppressed a sigh. I found I was already getting slightly deadened to the escalating sense of doom. I guess you really do find a point where it stops getting any worse, or at least it seems that way.

"I don't want to waste time with teasers, though, so let's just go and see, shall we?" he said, with a sweep of his arm toward the basement stairs.

Well, this could only get better, couldn't it?

He didn't say anything more as we descended into the basement. When we got down there, though, there wasn't really anything out of the ordinary; it was just a basement. Dusty furniture was clumped against the walls and a couple of bare light bulbs hung from sockets in the ceiling. There were no strange books, idols, symbols, or really anything that might suggest the supernatural or occult.

But Ashton didn't seem interested in anything in the basement. He was heading straight for the back wall.

There were a couple of old chairs against the wall that he slid out of the way. There was only one light in the basement, and it was over the stairs, so the back was dark enough that what he was looking for was not immediately obvious. Only as he reached into the recess in the wall did my eyes adjust to the dark enough to see the outline of a door. He turned a handle and pulled, and the door swung open, revealing at first only an empty blackness.

Instead of a flashlight, he used a lighter to light a candle that had apparently been set on one of the chairs, barely revealing a set of stairs curving downward in its flickering light. I thought it was overly theatrical, but I couldn't deny the sense of menace coming from that black hole in the ground. There was something bad down there, and I could feel it.

I glanced around me. Most of the students were shadowed enough that I couldn't see their expressions. A couple appeared eager, others just looked nervous. I caught a glimpse of Ari and the expression of sheer, pants-wetting terror in his eyes before he noticed me looking at him and clamped down on it.

So, I wasn't the only one who was less than enthusiastic about going down those stairs. There was a coldness seeping up from below, along with something like a smell, just below the threshold of detection. The more I tried to pin it down, quietly spreading my nostrils to try to sniff, the more it seemed to change. It smelled like rot, then like something musty and moldy, then it had a coppery smell, kind of like blood. Whatever it was, it smelled wrong.

But Ashton didn't seem to notice. Most of the other students, the ones who were crowding the closest to him, didn't seem to notice anything amiss, either. Without any further ado, he led the way down the steps.

The first thing I noticed once I was in the stairway was that it was not built like the rest of the house. The stairs were stone, not wood, metal, or concrete. The chill took hold shortly after crossing the threshold, and it was impossible to feel whether it was a dry or a damp chill. It was just enough to make you feel uncomfortable. It was like there was a layer of oily grit in the air that settled on my skin as I descended.

The stairs went deeper than might have been expected. When they ended, I began to see why.

At first, even though my eyes had further adjusted to the dark and the weak, flickering light of Ashton's candle, I couldn't see most of the room. The walls receded into pitch blackness above and to the sides. It wasn't so much a room as it was a vault.

In fact, as we spread out into the room, I saw that that was exactly what it was. The candle illuminated a squarish stone pillar rising up toward the ceiling, then another. It was a recreation of an old Gothic vault, for some reason buried under a Victorian-style house in central Colorado. Given everything else, I doubted the story behind its construction was anything so innocent as an eccentric millionaire with a taste for dark, Gothic architecture.

Ashton stopped about twenty feet into the vault and turned to face us, his features lit by the candle like something out of a cheesy horror movie. There was the vague suggestion of stacks of stuff behind him, but the light was too bad to tell what. "Yes, some of you may have noticed that this place looks a lot like a Gothic vault. And that's exactly what it is. What you can't see yet, since this candle is the only light down here at the moment, is what's in it. This first few feet is pretty open, but this place is *packed* with artifacts, books, and…other implements, all of which are of interest to our study." He looked around, spreading his arms wide to encompass the entire space. "It's going to take a long time to catalog all of it; probably longer than a semester. But I'm hoping that all of you are dedicated enough to the search for knowledge to stick with this project, because I'm fairly certain we just hit the mother-lode. To be sure, we're going to catalog a small portion of what I've looked at already, and then we're going to do another experiment."

Even as he said it, I got the crawling sensation of being watched, and I could have sworn that I caught a whiff of the sour vomit smell of the homunculus. I looked around, but there was no sign of it, or much of anything else. Anything could be hiding in the darkness around us.

Somehow, I got the sense that the homunculus, if it was there with us, was a relative newcomer, and not an entirely welcome one. That just made things even creepier. There were other things down there, inimical, watchful things that I couldn't see, and I doubted I'd necessarily be able to even if we got a million-candlepower floodlight down there.

"Come and see," Ashton said, and turned to go deeper into the vault. I couldn't think of anything I'd rather do less.

There were two tables and an armoire that came into focus first. The tables were intricately carved with legs that looked reptilian, but had too many toes. The top of one was white and porous-looking, as if it was made from bone. As I looked a little closer, I became convinced that it was, in fact, bone; it looked like a bunch of shoulder-blades carefully fitted together.

I didn't want to touch such a thing, but I did anyway. It sure felt like bone. It was also ice cold; colder than the rest of the room by far. I knew enough to know that that wasn't a good sign.

There were more candles on the tables, and Ashton lit them one by one. As he did, the museum of horror began to get clearer.

The bone table was littered with scrolls, ancient, musty-looking books, and various fetishes. One was obviously a severed, mummified human hand, with symbols tattooed into the waxy flesh. Another was a small statue made of what looked like clay, of something that managed to be formless and gruesome at one and the same time. There was the suggestion of tentacles and too many mouths, but the longer I looked at it, the less I could describe it. It was a lump of wrongness made manifest, sitting on a table apparently made from human bone.

And it wasn't even the most disturbing thing in the room that was being revealed by the growing candlelight.

There were more statues, most looking slightly warped in one way or another. One was flawless, a depiction of a young woman, except for what looked like blood splattered across her chest. Her eyes, instead of being sculpted, had been hollowed out into empty pits in the statue's face.

A display case, built of some sort of very dark wood that looked black in the dim light, stood up against one of the pillars. Every shelf was covered with masks, from wooden tribal masks to kabuki-style porcelain masks, to rubber theatrical makeup type masks. Only a few of them were obviously macabre, but all of them shared a certain disturbing quality. Some almost appeared to be watching, even though there were no eyes in the eyeholes.

Several paintings, some noticeably witchcraft-themed, lay on tables or were leaned up against pillars or cases. The paintings of witches and sorcerers conducting their dark arts weren't the creepy ones, though. Oh, no. The creepy ones were those that looked perfectly normal at first glance. The worst was one of a 17th-century aristocrat that looked innocent, if overly fat, when I was looking straight at it. But as soon as I saw it out of the corner of my eye, I caught a glimpse of the same man, but with five eyes, all leering at me, horns, three arms, and a second mouth growing out of his neck. As soon as I snapped my eyes back to look again, the painting was of the same serene, pudgy rich guy.

There were plenty of skulls; some plain, some adorned with symbols, or just gold and precious stones. A few more mummified or otherwise preserved body parts were in sight, mostly sitting on tables or shelves. A shriveled heart in a glass case was especially unnerving for some reason.

Don't even get me started on the damned dolls.

There was very little conversation as the rest of the students spread out through the lighted area, examining the various stacks of sinister curiosities. Ashton had stopped lighting candles, leaving much of the vault still in darkness. I wondered why, but it seemed pretty obvious that there was something more that he didn't necessarily want the class to see yet. He stood by a

95

case containing a mix of small goat-headed statues and books, and watched as the class examined the treasure-trove of occult objects. There was that feverish glint in his eyes again, even in the candlelight.

As I studied him, it occurred to me that there were almost two Clark Ashtons. There was the excitable, nerdy academic, and then there was the intense, feverishly obsessed occultist. There didn't seem to be much rhyme or reason as to which side was on top at any particular time.

It made him unpredictable, and I was sure it made him dangerous. There was a lot more going on under the surface than I'd seen before. I was beginning to wonder if he was entirely sane.

The entire vault seemed to have that same sort of elusive almost-smell that I'd detected at the top of the stairs. It was also cold, and not uniformly. Some of the objects had noticeably colder air around them than others.

It took me a few moments to get Ari's attention. Ashton wasn't staring at me specifically, but he was being quite attentive to the class as a whole, and I didn't want him to see what I was about to do. I hoped to get Ari to distract him, but the would-be Hunter was looking around, eyes wide, looking more than a little terrified. He'd been quite tough enough when he'd first showed up at class, but that was before things started getting real.

Now, his façade was cracking. It was putting the entire case at risk, but he was the only close support I had down here, and I hoped that getting him involved might help break him out of his terror, and hopefully keep him focused enough to not give us away.

I got his attention, finally. I was about to walk up to him and just tell him to go talk to Ashton and keep him busy, but he finally looked over and met my eyes. I looked over toward Ashton, saw he wasn't looking my way, and tilted my head in his direction. When I looked back at Ari, he swallowed, then nodded, squared his shoulders, and stepped over to the professor.

I didn't know what he was going to come up with to talk about; Ari had never been all that engaged in the classes. It didn't matter to me, as long as he kept Ashton busy while I did my thing.

I waited, carefully watching the two of them out of the corner of my eye as I made it look like I was intently studying one of the scrolls on the bone table. Once Ashton stopped looking around and fixed his gaze on Ari, I carefully glanced around to see if any of the other students were looking. All were absorbed in the vault's macabre contents, and not really paying attention to each other. The effeminate guy I'd disliked from the get-go, Trevor, and his two lady-friends were the only ones talking, in excited whispers. Everyone else was subdued. I think a few were getting creeped out by their surroundings. Even the Goth kids were quiet and nervous.

I slipped my steel flask of holy water out of my back pocket, and, keeping it in the shadows—an easy enough task in the dim candlelight—I quietly opened it, shaking a few drops out onto my fingers. I shook them onto the scroll in front of me in the Sign of the Cross.

There was no action or sound in response. The cold around the table seemed to subside, just a little bit. And the feeling of menace in the shadows around us seemed to heighten.

Keeping the flask just inside my open flannel shirt, I worked my way around the lighted area. I didn't move any faster than the rest of the students; that would have attracted attention. I was pretty sure I had *something*'s attention, but for the moment, whatever was hiding in the dark, or in plain sight among the artifacts, was biding its time. But I got more and more certain that I was being watched as I splashed drops of holy water on several of the more gruesome artifacts, as well as a few that showed the greatest tendency to change when no one was looking straight at them. I didn't look at the shifting painting of the aristocrat when I flicked four drops of holy water at it, but I could almost swear I heard an enraged scream, faintly, like it came from a great distance, as I did.

As I got closer to the case full of masks, I noticed the girl standing in front of it wasn't looking too good. Her name was Sandy, I remembered that much. She wasn't bad looking, if a few pounds overweight. But right now, she was staring wide-eyed at the case, pale and starting to shake. I could hear her breathing speeding up as I got closer. She was already borderline hyperventilating. I'm no shrink, but I know a panic attack when I see one.

I stepped closer, and gently touched her elbow. She started like a scared rabbit, turning to face me. She didn't bolt, but she was shaking. "Are you all right?" I asked, already knowing the answer. It seemed kind of trite, but that's what you ask in those sorts of situations, I guess.

"I don't like it down here," she said in a loud, frightened whisper. "I…I have to get out of here. I can't take this…I feel like something bad is going to happen."

It was entirely possible that she was very right about that, but it wasn't the time or the place to say that. "Okay," I said. "Let's get you out of here. I've got a light; we can go upstairs." I did have a small, powerful flashlight in my pocket, along with my Colt in my waistband behind my back.

I glanced over at Ashton, but Ari had managed to get him thoroughly involved in conversation. He wasn't looking around at us, but was absorbed in what Ari was saying, his feverishly intent gaze fixed on the other man's face. I steered Sandy toward the stairs.

We got there without incident. I was glad that the candlelight extended to the portal, though the stairway itself was still pitch black. The sense of oppressive malevolence coming from the darkened parts of the vault had intensified as I'd started us toward the exit. I got the distinct impression that something down there didn't want us to leave.

I took the chance, and waited until we had gone around a turn on the stairs before I switched on my flashlight. I didn't know how Ashton would react if he noticed us leaving, and a one hundred eighty lumen light would probably attract his attention.

As we mounted the steps, I kept my hand on Sandy's elbow, more as reassurance than anything else, though I wanted to be able to catch her if she fell. She was stumbling a little as we went up the stairs, her breath still coming in rapid pants, and a little bit of a whimper escaping every once in a while. The girl was terrified.

When we got to the top of the stairs, I paused, holding her back. She strained against my grip, whimpering a little more loudly; she wanted out of there. But I wanted to make sure that we weren't walking into an ambush in the basement. I was under no illusions, even then, that the things in the vault were all necessarily confined there.

I stood in the doorway and flashed the light around the room. A couple of shadows seemed to move in a way that didn't match the movement of the flashlight beam, but nothing else appeared. I cautiously moved into the room, Sandy close on my heels. Old habits from the desert were coming back. The closer we got to being home free, the more I expected the worst to happen.

But we crossed the basement floor without incident, heading up the stairs to the ground floor. I still didn't relax.

Finally, we were at the front door. Once we were outside, standing on the porch, I turned to face Sandy, and took her by the shoulders.

"Sandy, listen to me," I said. "You need to get far away from this house, and never come back. Do you understand? Just get away."

She finally looked me in the eyes. "What he's doing… what they're all doing…it's dangerous, isn't it?"

I nodded. "Yeah, it is. A lot more dangerous than they realize."

"So are you leaving, too?" she asked.

I shook my head. "I can't. I've got work to do. This kind of thing is sort of my job now." I looked back at the house. You know the pictures of haunted houses, where the windows look like evil eyes, staring at you? Well, the windows behind me, looking out on the porch, were starting to feel like eyes, staring at us. I wasn't sure how much of it was just my imagination; it was possible that this continuous exposure to the uncanny was doing things to my perception, but I somehow doubted it. "I have to. You don't. Get away, and *don't ever come back.*"

She looked like she was going to argue for about half a second. Then she looked back at the house, apparently changed her mind, and hurried down the porch steps, out the gate, and down the street. I stepped out to the gate to watch her, in case something, like the homunculus, decided to pop out and go after her, but nothing materialized. Sending up a quick prayer for her safety, I turned and headed back into the heart of darkness.

I carefully eased back into the mix down in the vault. The atmosphere hadn't changed much; everyone was still taking everything in. Ari was stepping away from Ashton, who was

99

looking around the class and rubbing his hands together. It looked like he was getting ready to start moving on.

He stopped. "Where's Sandy?" he asked.

Crap. "She wasn't feeling well," I said. "I helped her upstairs and got her on her way home." It was technically the truth.

He frowned. "That's unfortunate," he said. He sounded distracted. I wondered which part was "unfortunate;" the fact that she hadn't been feeling well, or the fact that I'd gotten her out of there.

"All right, then," he said. "Tonight, we're just going to do some familiarization with the artifacts in this little area, here. Rest assured, there is a *lot* more down here. But we're going to start cataloguing what is here, and cross-referencing some of the older pieces with the *Codex*." He looked around with that disturbingly intense expression again. "This stuff is for real, but how much is really going to be useful is what we have to find out."

"Excuse me, professor?" one of the other students ventured. I didn't remember the kid's name. "Useful for what? I mean, I guess I knew we were trying to learn about the occult, but it sounds like you've got something more…I don't know… *specific* in mind."

Ashton's gaze flicked over quickly, his eyes burning. "I might," he said finally, after staring at the student for a long, uncomfortable moment. Obsessive, crazy Ashton was at the fore that night. "It's…complicated. I don't know that I should say what it is, until I can figure out exactly if we have everything we'll need to pursue it." He flashed a grin, trying to look like the eager, nerdy professor, but it looked more like a skull's rictus than a boyish grin. "Rest assured, when it comes together—*if* it comes together—it will be very, very illuminating."

I'll just bet, I thought. I wondered how far I should let this go before I took action. But Dan's words about keeping force as a last resort kept echoing in my mind, even then. If there was a chance that I could simply turn this aside, I had to take it. Unfortunately, that meant biding my time until I saw an opening, and there certainly didn't appear to be one at the moment.

Later on, as I gained more experience, I would have been more decisive. But I was still feeling my way along at that point.

As much as I instinctively wanted to strike, I wasn't sure exactly when I'd be justified in doing so.

"So," he said, turning and picking up the heavy book that I recognized as the *Codex*, "Let's start closest to the door, and work our way clockwise. Get settled in, folks, this could take a while."

The class took on the character of an archaeological survey, albeit one increasingly hunched against the malevolent scrutiny of things that could be neither seen nor heard. The sense of oppression coming from the darkness only got more acute as the next couple hours went on, as much as everyone tried to ignore it and concentrate on cataloguing the objects and books in the room. Ashton got everyone gathered together, concentrating on one thing at a time, standing in a tight circle around him and the book, and whichever table or case he was concentrating on at the time.

This had the effect of putting everyone's backs to the darkness. I wasn't the only one uncomfortable with this; I noticed several others glancing over their shoulders at the shadows. I doubt any of them knew just what was bothering them, but the sense of being watched by *something* was getting stronger and stronger the longer we stayed down there.

Finally, after about two hours, it got to be too much for several of them. A few of the other students started muttering amongst themselves. At the center of the small knot of students, two guys and three girls, was Sean, a fit younger guy who'd never said much in class, but had always been attentive. Ari was the other guy.

I eased closer to them. The little knot of people was the closest group to the stairs, and some of them were already starting to drift toward them. The nervous glances at the darkened parts of the vault were getting more frequent, too.

It was Sean who finally broached the subject. "Uh, professor?" he ventured. "It's getting awfully late, and some of us have class in the morning...I think we should wrap this up for tonight and go."

Ashton looked at him like he'd just suggested burning the Mona Lisa. Sean held up his watch. "It's getting close to midnight."

Ashton just frowned. "This is important," he said. "I don't know why you'd want to leave early." He waved his hand to encompass the vault. "We still have a lot of work to do here. We've just gotten started."

"And we can come back and continue later," Sean pointed out. "None of this is going anywhere."

Ashton's frown was deepening into real anger. It looked like obsessive, not entirely sane Ashton wasn't going away that night. "You mean to tell me that none of you have ever stayed up until five in the morning partying and then gone to class anyway?" he demanded. "But when there's work involved, you want to leave because it's 'getting late?'" He shook his head in disgust. "Fine, get out of here. Maybe we'll find the key piece of the puzzle without you."

I met Ari's earnest glance, and nodded fractionally. I'd leave with them. I didn't know why, but I suddenly had the feeling that I was supposed to, that they'd need me with them.

We headed up the stairs as a group. I stayed in the shadows of the rest of the group as much as possible; I didn't want Ashton to see me go and kick up a fuss about it. We made our way up the stairs and through the basement.

There was something different about the basement when we came out of the stairwell. Even with more than one flashlight, the place looked dim, dark. None of the lights seemed to be shining as brightly as they should. There seemed to always be something moving out of the corner of my eye, but when I turned to look there was nothing. "Come on," I said, the first words I'd spoken since I'd told Sandy not to return. "We need to get out of here, pronto."

I looked at the stairs, and was sure I saw a figure move there, but when I swung my flashlight on it, there was nothing. I didn't know if there was such a thing as shadow-people, though I'd heard a few stories about them, but that had looked like the shadow of a person, standing by the stairs.

I briefly considered bringing my Colt out, but there was nothing to shoot at yet, and I figured that presenting a pistol was only going to freak my companions out even more, so I left it in my waistband.

We hurried up the stairs in a tight, nervous group. I had sort of bulled my way to the front, not out of necessarily more of a hurry to get away from the vault, but because I expected I was the only one armed, and I get paranoid about ambushes when trying to get out of an unpleasant situation. If I was up front, I had a better chance of dealing with anything that might be lying in wait for us as we left.

I swept the light across the room at the top of the steps. There was still that nagging sense of movement not quite entirely seen, but nothing popped out to jump us. I pushed forward toward the living room, the other five close on my heels.

As I crossed the threshold into the living room, I heard a distinct, loud whisper that nevertheless was completely unintelligible. I looked back at the rest of them, but they were wide-eyed, scared, and obviously none of them had made a sound.

Great. Things were getting weird, Ari looked just as terrified as the rest of them, and I was essentially on my own. As I turned back toward the front door, one of the shadows passed right in front of my flashlight beam. It was against the wall, where a shadow was supposed to be, but there was nothing to cast it. I pushed on toward the door. There was no guarantee that outside was any safer than inside, but I didn't see how it could necessarily be that worse.

Someday I'll stop thinking such idiotic thoughts.

As we stepped out onto the porch, the yard almost looked like it was alive with shifting shadows. There was hardly any wind, so what we were seeing couldn't be put down to waving branches. There were a couple of glimmers under the trees that might have been fireflies, except they came in pairs, and looked disturbingly like eyes.

None of that was the worst of it, though. That came when six figures walked out of the shadows on the street and gathered at the gate. They were on two legs and had two arms, but they weren't human. Their legs were bent the wrong way, and they had heads like goats.

They came through the gate with a bleating yell and charged the porch.

Chapter 9

Now, Dan had mentioned fighting a goathead, but I realized he hadn't said much about just how to deal with them. At that point, I wasn't worried about it; I had come to accept that there was going to be a lot I didn't know for a while. I *was* worried about whether or not the silver-jacketed hollow points in my Colt were going to have more effect on these things than they'd had on the homunculus.

My 1911 was an older one, and I'd always been too cheap or too poor to upgrade it. So it still had the basic blade sights that the model had had as far back as World War II—no fancy tritium night sights. Fortunately, I had a powerful flashlight in my off hand.

I pinned the first goat-headed thing in the brilliant white circle of light, lined the sights up, and shot it in the face just before it mounted the stairs. It's head jerked back, dark tissue splashed from the wound, and it dropped backwards off the steps. It landed hard and didn't move.

The rest stopped dead in their tracks. The noise of the shot had been strangely deadened, but so had the yelling of the weird, goat-headed things. There was no echo; it was like sound wasn't escaping the yard. It was eerily similar to the strange sound distortion on Powell Hill a few nights back.

As I swung the light and the pistol barrel away from the dead thing lying on the ground at the base of the steps, the rest backed away. They muttered and bleated, none of it making much sense, and tried to stay away from the light. It seemed like it was having a harsher effect than just the brightness hurting dark-adjusted eyes; they seemed to find the touch of the light itself to be painful. As I swung the light on one, it dodged behind a tree. I switched to the next and it flinched, trying to scurry backward into the hedge.

They were spreading out into a semi-circle around the porch. Two were stationed by the gate, flinching but still standing their ground when I turned the light on them. I couldn't keep it on them very long, since as soon as I moved it away from the steps, another one would try to advance.

"Ari," I called, "Where's your gun?"

"I...I don't have one," he stammered.

"What? You don't have one?" I couldn't help myself; I snapped my head around to glare at him, but had to turn back to aim at another goathead that was starting to jump toward the porch. It backed off. *What kind of Hunter—even a wannabe— didn't have a gun?*

"I'm not really any good with them," he tried to explain, the pitch of his voice rising. There was pure, unadulterated terror in his voice.

Great. I was alone, with a handful of terror-stricken college students huddled behind me, against a bunch of otherworldly creatures, with one gun and eight rounds left in the mag. Fortunately, the goatheads appeared to react quite satisfyingly to bullets.

Still, it was only a matter of time before they rushed the porch. When that happened, I was going to run out of ammo fast. For the moment, I was holding them off by the reality that the first one to step up was going to go the way of the one at the base of the stairs...I glanced down at it briefly, only to see it rapidly decomposing already. I hadn't known Otherworlders did that.

There was a patter of footsteps, and a shriek from one of the girls. I whirled, to see another goathead trying to climb the banister behind us, reaching for the other girl. I didn't have a great shot, especially with most of the knot of students between me and the target, but I lined it up and fired as the girls shrank back against the wall. The students flinched away from the muzzle blast and the goathead tumbled off the porch with a yelp.

I whirled back to the steps and fired again, the muzzle only inches from the next goathead's nose. Hot blood spattered on my hand, and the creature dropped like a rock.

The crowd backed off a little more, holding by the trees and the hedge, still trying to avoid my light. I knew I'd have to do something soon; the batteries in that light weren't going to last forever, and while I didn't have an exact count, I was pretty sure there were still more of those things out there in the dark than I had rounds left in my pistol.

I took a step down the stairs. The nearest goathead flinched back as I pointed light and gun at it.

A weird, bleating voice sounded through the dark. "You are one of *His* servants," it said accusingly. "You defile the relics, affront against the Great Ones. You must die. All who defy the Great Ones must die."

"Don't know who the 'great ones' are," I said, "and I don't care. But I am one of His servants." I gripped the light in the fingers of my gun hand, and reached into my shirt to pull out the silver crucifix and let it hang on my chest.

The effect was electric. The closest goathead shrieked and scampered toward the gate. A couple of its fellows stampeded along with it, and there was a scuffle. Apparently the two at the gate weren't ready to retreat yet. The runners won the argument, though, and in a few moments the yard was empty, the goatheads having all run out into the darkened street.

I cautiously continued down the steps, scanning every corner of the yard. I paused at the bottom, standing over the disintegrating corpse of the third goathead I'd shot, and quickly reloaded before starting across the yard. My flashlight and gun muzzle went everywhere my eyes went. No goatheads appeared, though a few of the shadows did still seem to shift in ways the movement of my light couldn't account for. I thought I could still hear the whispering, too, though that might have just been the wind.

It took a while to cross the yard, stepping cautiously and slowly. I didn't believe for a heartbeat that the night's horrors were over. While nothing came after us in the yard, when I got to the gate, I could see furtive movement down the street, and I was pretty sure the goatheads hadn't gone far.

Fortunately, the direction I wanted to go looked clear, though the streetlights were distressingly dim and far apart. There was a time when I wouldn't have thought that was a drawback, but that was before all the nasties *lived* in the dark.

I got through the gate and stepped toward where I'd seen the movement, my pistol at low ready, and hissed at the students behind me, "Come on!" They shuffled through. If they hadn't been crowding so close behind me, I don't think they would have been able to make it across the yard from the porch at that point. They were in shock; even Ari wasn't looking too good. Ari hadn't seen much of this stuff for real before Powell Hill, and the rest hadn't even really imagined it existed, or if they had, they hadn't expected it to be like this.

Once all of them were out of the yard, I said, "Follow me," and headed down the street, away from the goatheads and toward the Church. The parish priest might not have been receptive to the idea that there was a problem with people dabbling in the occult on campus, but I wanted to get these kids on holy ground. I didn't know for sure how well that would work, but it seemed like a good idea.

As I trotted down the street with my little flock in tow, I grumbled, "Doesn't this town have any cops? Gunshots, goat-men yelling, and now a man running down the street with a pistol out, and there's nothing?"

"Whoever summoned these creatures must have taken measures that it wouldn't be noticed, or couldn't be responded to," Ari huffed from the back. He sounded a little bit more collected than he had back on the porch, so that was good. "I'd be willing to bet that phones and radios aren't working right. It sounded like sound was muffled back at the house, too, so people may not even have noticed."

"That does not sound like a good thing," I said.

"It's not," he replied. "In most cases I've heard of, it means there is something very, very powerful involved."

"Great," I said, and kept moving. I glanced back frequently, catching several glimpses of goat-ish shapes flitting from shadow to shadow. I hadn't scared them off; they were following us.

There were other things out there, as well. The shadows continued to shift and move on their own, and there was always the suggestion of other things following us, things that I could only see out of the corner of my eye. As soon as I looked directly at them, they were gone.

One of the girls screamed again. When I looked over, she was several steps away from the rest of the pack, but running back to it. "Something grabbed me!" she gasped. I shone my light toward where she'd been, but there was nothing there.

"Keep moving," I said. "Stay together and move quickly." I briefly thought about Sandy, and prayed she'd gotten away safely. If this had been going on when I sent her home, she could still be out here somewhere, snatched up by whatever was lurking in the dark.

Fortunately, the church wasn't that far away. There was even a pair of orange-glowing streetlights out on the sidewalk in front of it. As soon as I got under one of them, I shoved the nearest student toward the front doors. "Go on, get inside, quick!" I told him. "They shouldn't be able to come after us in there." I was spitballing, but it seemed logical at the time.

I stayed where I was, facing back toward the house. The darkness seemed to be alive. The goatheads continued to flit from tree to tree, their eyes occasionally glinting in the light spilling from the streetlights. Other, formless things that I couldn't ever quite see clearly moved in the dark, invisible except for their stirrings, which drew the eye without anything being there to focus on.

And further back down the street, behind all of the seething strangeness, there was a short, large-headed silhouette, just standing there.

My blood ran cold at the sight of it. I imagined I caught a whiff of the sour stink that followed that shape. I could almost see that creepy, idiot grin. It was well beyond pistol range, not that shooting it would have done anything useful in the first place.

What was pulling that thing's strings? Was it really Ashton? As manic and obsessive as he seemed to be, it just didn't seem to fit. I didn't think he was telling the whole story about his "search for knowledge" in the vault, but he'd been blindsided by the failure of the ritual on Powell Hill. It just didn't seem to me like he was powerful enough to be the guiding hand behind that thing.

Behind me, I heard the door rattle, then somebody started pounding on it. I glanced back, to see Ari tugging hard, and increasingly frantically, on the church's door handles. It was locked.

"Rectory's around the side," I told him. "Go wake the Father up." Ari ran around the corner, while the rest huddled on the church's front steps and stared out at the night. There was a lot of white showing in their eyes.

I was starting to wonder where Dan was. I knew he hadn't parked far away; he was always staying in the neighborhood as backup. But I hadn't seen his truck on the way to the church, and there was no sign of him approaching. I didn't have a cell phone, and I was pretty sure Dan didn't, either. We might have to do something about that, provided I survived the night.

Even from around the corner, I could hear Ari beating on the priest's door. There was no response for a long time, while the shadows seemed to grow deeper and the flickers of movement drew nearer. The streetlight I was standing under seemed to flicker and get dimmer.

Ari's pounding stopped, and muffled voices from around the corner suggested that the priest had finally answered the door. At the same time, headlights came around the corner from behind me and lit up the goatheads and the homunculus, which was now standing in the middle of the street, about two blocks away, watching us.

Dan's Bronco roared up to the curb in front of the church. Father Ignacio's bike was right behind it. I backed up to the truck as Dan got out, his .50 Beowulf in one hand and my .45-70 in the other. I hastily holstered my pistol and reached my hand out for the rifle. He tossed it to me; I caught it and checked it. It was loaded, though there wasn't a round in the chamber. I worked the lever and reached into the passenger seat, where he'd tossed my cartridge belt.

I felt better able to deal with the goatheads now, but that homunculus wasn't going to be any more responsive to bullets than it had been at Ray's ranch. "Did you bring a flamethrower, by any chance?" I asked.

"No, I don't have one of those handy," he replied. "There's a crate of Molotovs in the back, though, and the butane torch is still in there, too, if it gets that close."

I glanced back, to see a case of glass bottles with oily rags sticking out of their necks. "That's definitely better than nothing," I said.

Father Ignacio had swung off his bike and walked up to stand next to me. He didn't have a weapon, aside from the large, twelve-inch-tall crucifix in his hand. Somehow I didn't worry about him. Aside from the air of absolute confidence he had about him and that crucifix, he just looked hard enough to take a few goatheads apart with his bare hands.

The local priest didn't seem to notice the strangeness out in the night. He just saw a bunch of terrified college students demanding access to the church at first.

"What is going on here?" he demanded. "Why do you need to get in the church? It's late. Is this some kind of prank? Are you kids drunk?" Then he apparently noticed the three older men with weapons standing on the sidewalk. He stopped where he was, and took a step back. I looked over at him and saw the fear in his face. "Okay," he said, trying to buy some time to get his thoughts together. I could see he'd nearly pissed himself at the sight of our rifles. "Let's everyone just stay calm. There's no need for anyone to get hurt. Just let us go inside, all right?"

He thought we were either criminals or nutjobs with guns. I was about to say something when Sean interjected. "No, Father, those guys aren't the ones we're worried about. It's *them*." He pointed out into the darkness.

The priest's eyes obviously hadn't adjusted to the darkness yet. He peered out into the dark, but the streetlights were doing a good job of obscuring the movement in the shadows. The homunculus and a few of the goatheads were still visible in the glare of Dan's headlights, though. And, whether driven by the homunculus or for some other reason, the goatheads were starting to run toward us.

He started to say something about calling the police, just as a shrill, bleating yell went up from the street. I couldn't make out what they were shouting, but it started to sound like a name, yelled over and over. It was garbled and unintelligible, but even what I could make out of it was distinctly unpleasant, rather like listening to fingernails scraped across a chalkboard.

The priest's protests were immediately pushed out of my mind. I shouldered my rifle and got ready for the rush.

I was pretty sure there were more than there had been in the yard. They came out of the shadows along the street in a mob, illuminated by the headlights and the spillover from the streetlights. I put the rifle's gold bead on the closest one and stroked the trigger.

My .45-70 and Dan's .50 thundered almost as one. Father Ignacio stepped between us, facing the onrushing mob, and raised that big crucifix of his. He started to pray in Latin, his gravelly voice rolling across the street, somehow still audible over the gunfire.

I could have sworn that the crucifix started giving off light of its own. At the very least, it seemed to catch every bit of the light from the headlights and reflected it outward with a brilliant white glare. The front rank of goatheads were blinking and flinching, slowing down in the face of that silvery gleam.

Two of them had dropped like rocks when Dan and I fired, smashed off their feet by the impacts of the big bullets. I rocked the lever, while Dan simply shifted targets and fired again. He wasn't that far ahead of me, though. I was still getting used to it, but that lever-action was pretty smooth.

For a few moments, the street was a cacophony of gunfire, roared Latin prayer, and bleating, shrieking yells. Much like back in the yard, they weren't trying a straight-up rush once the first few went down. They milled about, trying to get back out of the headlights, and tried to spread out to flank us.

There were a lot of them. I stopped shooting as soon as they stopped advancing, and shoved a couple of rounds into the loading port. They kept spreading out, many all but disappearing into the darkness beyond the headlights. I still had my flashlight in my off hand, pressed against the rifle's forearm, and I turned it on, pointed along the barrel. I followed several of the goatheads as they circled us.

"We're going to be surrounded pretty soon," I pointed out.

"Yeah, we are," Dan concurred. "We need to fall back to the church. I'm pretty sure the homunculus at least won't be able to follow us in there."

"What about the goathead things?" I asked. We were facing nearly opposite directions now, trying to keep enough of the goatheads covered that none of them would want to chance charging us. One started to, though, along with a handful of his cronies. I saw the movement start out of the corner of my eye, whirled, and fired.

They were fast; the thing was barely thirty feet away when I blasted it. The big bullet took it high in the chest and it fell on its face. I worked the lever and shot the next one behind it as it tried to skid to a halt and backpedal. Even in the dark and feeling shaky and terrified, it's hard to miss at thirty feet, especially if you know your way around a gun, which I daresay I do.

"They're idiots," Father Ignacio paused his litany just long enough to say. "Low-intelligence tools of greater forces. They might still try it, though they're usually too terrified to try to run onto holy ground. If there's something scary enough pushing them, though, they'll try."

The homunculus was still standing in the headlights back there, not advancing, just standing there staring. I was pretty sure that it, or whatever was controlling it, qualified as "scary enough."

"Ari!" I yelled over my shoulder. "Grab that crate full of bottles from the back, and get everybody inside!" I didn't dare chance a glance back at the priest, but I heard Ari call out that he understood, and his footsteps behind me, followed by the faint rattle of the crate being lifted out of the Bronco's back hatch.

"Come on!" I recognized Sean's voice. A quick glance over my shoulder showed that the church doors were open, and most of the students had run inside. Sean was pulling the priest, who looked almost catatonic, through the doorway. Ari was running up the steps with the crate full of Molotov cocktails.

I had to turn back and shoot another goathead that had decided to take advantage of my momentary distraction to try to run at me. The big bullet took half its head off. These things might be mean, but they were pretty fragile when it came down to it. Of course, there were a lot more of them than there were of us.

112

"We're going to have to run for it," Dan called from behind me, after another pair of shots *boomed* in the night. "They're going to rush us as soon as they see an opening. When I say 'go,' run for the doors."

I shot another that tried to come from the corner of the church while I was looking across the street. "Waiting on you," I replied.

"Now!" he shouted. I turned on my heel and sprinted for the steps.

It was a short run, but the goatheads were on our heels when we got to the doors. I hit the doorframe and pivoted, bringing my rifle up and squeezing the trigger. The flame spat from the muzzle with a thunderous report, blasting a silver-jacketed round straight into the nearest goathead's eye.

There was a bit of a traffic jam at the door, as all three of us arrived at pretty much the same moment. Dan and I kind of shoved Father Ignacio inside behind us, and opened fire on the mob of goatheads that had come bounding out of the dark as soon as our backs were turned.

For a moment, the night was nothing but gunfire and screaming. The bleating screams were muted compared to the thunder of our two rifles, but there was enough of it that it was still audible. That street was a nightmare of stabbing flame, unholy noise, and unnatural bloodlust.

And through it all, that freakish, doll-like figure stayed where it was, still in the light of Dan's headlights, though the light flickered as goatheads ran in front of it, still staring, that imbecilic grin still splitting its face.

While it felt like an eternity of noise and violence, it could only have been a couple of heartbeats before Father Ignacio got his equilibrium, straightened, and shoved between us, that big silver crucifix held out at arm's length, the Latin litany rolling off his tongue. The crucifix blazed again, like it was gathering every bit of ambient light and amplifying it.

The goatheads fell back, squealing in dismay. They had all but halted in the face of our storm of gunfire, but it was that crucifix that finally broke them. They didn't vanish, though. They retreated back to the other side of the street, but they stayed there, milling about and still muttering that hideous name.

Down the street, the homunculus sketched a jerky, puppet-on-a-string wave, and walked off, disappearing into the dark.

As the night wore on and dawn approached, Dan and I took turns at the door, while Father Ignacio saw to the students, and the local priest. Father James was starting to recover from the shock of what he'd seen, but he was still in denial, despite Father Ignacio's gruff assurances that he hadn't imagined any of it. The older, grizzled priest finally hauled him to an open window and pointed out the goatheads across the street.

He still didn't want to believe it. There had to be another explanation. I left him to Father Ignacio's ministrations and took my place again at the door.

The first light of dawn was just starting to turn the eastern horizon gray. The shadows were still alive in the twilight, shifting and staying darker than they should have. The darkness didn't want to give way to morning any sooner than it had to. The goatheads were still there, lurking in the deeper shadows, still quietly chanting that name. There was an insidious sort of horror to the sound; while the name remained unintelligible, the sound had an effect all by itself. When I caught myself listening to it, all sorts of gruesome, macabre images started springing to mind. It reminded me of the night in the desert, and the dark, twisted mental shadow that had preceded the ifrit's attack. It wasn't all that audible inside, so Dan and I had quietly agreed to make sure the rest of the students, including Ari, stayed away from the door as much as possible.

Still, there was a comfort to be found, staying inside the church. For all the horror outside, there was sanctuary there, a quiet sort of reminder, if I had the presence of mind to notice, that the things out there couldn't touch us under the eyes of the big crucifix on the wall.

As I watched the Otherworld prowl and slink in the dark, I realized that it wasn't just the goatheads muttering that name. The whispers that had dogged us all the way from the house were murmuring it, too.

"Have you heard that before?" I asked Dan. "Or heard of it?"

He shook his head, still watching the street. "Can't say as I have," he replied. "I think if we could make it out, we might have an idea of who or what is pulling the strings. That's definitely not Ashton's name."

I nodded agreement. While I had realized that Ashton was definitely more than he first appeared, I still had the nagging thought that he was, ultimately, a tool. A willing tool, perhaps, but still a tool. The question was, a tool for who...or what?

Chapter 10

As the morning light grew stronger, the shadows faded. The sinister movement beneath the trees across the street was replaced by the waving of tree branches in the gentle morning breeze, and the goatheads disappeared with the shadows. The whispering and muttering was gone by the time dawn broke.

I stayed by the door with Dan, rifle still in hand, watching as the Otherworld retreated before the light of day. Father Ignacio had the students and Father James gathered around him. He was talking to them about what had happened and what they had seen. His voice was pitched low enough that I couldn't make out most of what he was saying, but he was surprisingly gentle and reassuring, given his appearance. He looked even more like a Hell's Angel or cartel sicario in the dark than he had in the daytime.

"I'm going to have to go back to that house," I said quietly, still watching where I'd last seen a goathead.

Dan just nodded. "I'll keep closer this time. What's your plan?"

I took a deep breath. Truth be told, I wasn't anxious to go back. "I've got to try to talk him down. I don't think it'll work; he's pretty committed to this little project of his. But I've got to try." I think I was trying to convince myself as much as anything else at that point. "If I can show him that someone or something's been using him, maybe that will open his eyes."

"And if it doesn't? Or if there is no guiding hand, and he's actually doing this all by his own initiative?"

There it was. If I couldn't get him to see the light, if he was well and truly committed to congress with the Abyss, was I ready to take violent action to stop him?

I wasn't constitutionally opposed to violence. I'd been a Marine, for crying out loud. I'd fired plenty of rounds in anger in Iraq. I knew I'd killed people, people who were trying to kill me and my fellow Marines.

But this was something else, at least that was the way it seemed to me. The night before had showed, more than anything else, that the dangers of trifling with the supernatural were very, very real. But would Ashton, if it came to that, fight? Would he give me a clear and present threat to neutralize? Or would I have to shoot him in cold blood? Even after everything I'd seen, I didn't like that option. It felt too much like murder.

"I'll deal with that when I come to it," I said. I didn't want to commit myself more than that, at least not until I'd confronted Ashton. Dan kept his peace and just nodded.

I glanced back at the rest of the students, but they were focused on Father Ignacio. The sun was almost up, most of the shadows had vanished, and if I was going to catch Ashton, I'd have to go soon. I still wasn't exactly comfortable going back up that street on my own in the early light of day; after the night before I still wasn't convinced that there wasn't anything else still lurking out there. The demon in the Drop Inn had manifested in broad daylight, after all.

But procrastinating wasn't going to make the task go away. It would probably just make it harder. I handed my rifle and bandolier back to Dan, and started down the steps.

Halfway down, I stopped and turned. Dan was still standing there in the door, my rifle out of sight, but his held ready. "What about Ari?" I asked.

Dan's mouth thinned. "I'll talk to him. Father Ignacio probably will, too; he's run into him before. We'll get him a place doing book research or something. We do have to make sure he doesn't try to fumble around in the field anymore. I've got a couple ideas." He nodded to me. "Don't worry about him.

Worry about what you've got to do. I'll make sure he doesn't get in your way." That was as good as I could hope for; I nodded and continued down the steps.

It was a cold morning. Fall was definitely in full swing. My breath smoked as I walked to Dan's truck, opened the back, and pulled out a couple of boxes of .45. I re-loaded the partially-spent pistol mag I'd used at the house, then slid it back into the mag holder on my belt. I did this almost on automatic, my eyes constantly scanning the street.

Finally, with my magazines topped off, I didn't have anything else to keep me close to the church. Even if Father James had a hard time accepting that evil is very real and very tangible, in ways that most people never get to see, just being close to a church had been comforting. Now I was heading back to that house, along with whatever was lurking in and below it. I hadn't seen the homunculus out in the daylight yet, but somehow I doubted it was going to be bound by the hours of darkness. And, again, I didn't have much of anything to burn it with.

On that thought, I turned back to the truck and rummaged around in one of the duffel bags in the back, until I found the butane torch Dan had mentioned. I pulled it out, then realized I had nowhere to put it. Just walking in with a torch wasn't going to look right, and I didn't usually carry a backpack. I found one on the floor, though, dropped the torch into it, and slung it over my shoulder. I'd leave it by the porch when I got there; I just hoped that if I needed it, I could get clear to grab it before something else grabbed me.

Finally satisfied that I was as ready as I was going to get, I slammed the truck door and started down the street. It was still early enough that the sound of the door slamming echoed up and down the street, almost making me flinch with how loud it sounded. The contrast with the deadened cacophony of malicious noise battling prayer and gunfire from the hours of darkness was striking.

I walked back the few short blocks to the house like a man marching to the gallows. No one else stirred; it was still pretty early. Granted, not much stirs near a college campus before eight in the morning, but it still seemed eerily quiet.

When I got to the house, there was no sign that anything had happened the night before. There were no bodies, no bloodstains, nothing. Well, not exactly nothing. As I mounted the steps to the porch, I saw a couple of my spent .45 casings on the boards, and there was a mushroomed, silver-jacketed .45 hollow point on the ground at the foot of the steps, where the first goathead I'd shot had fallen. There was no sign of the corpse, and no tissue left on the bullet. I couldn't even explain why it was there, instead of somewhere in the bushes after it had blown through the goathead's skull. I'd been sure I'd seen the splash of an exit wound.

On impulse, I scooped up the casings and the bullet, dropping them in my pocket. I didn't know if there might be some investigation of the events the previous night; I still didn't have any idea why no one had called the police after the first couple of gunshots. If someone had called after dawn had sent the sinister forces in the dark packing, it probably wouldn't be a good idea to have evidence of my having discharged a firearm on campus lying around. Still, there were no sirens, and no police cars in sight.

I was sure that Ashton must have finished up and sent the rest of the class home while we'd held our ground on the church steps. But when I stepped inside, they were just then coming up out of the basement. It had evidently been a long night for them, as well. Just about every eye was red-rimmed with fatigue. Most of them looked a little bit out of it, too, and not just from being tired, either. There was disquiet and horror in a few of those glances, but it was deep down, masked by curiosity or academic enthusiasm.

I wanted to shake them. I wanted to tell them to get away, to try to forget about this stuff. I knew it wasn't really going to work; if my own experiences were anything to go on, even if you did try to walk away, once you'd engaged in this stuff, it stayed after you. There wasn't any going back once you'd seen beyond the veil.

They kind of shuffled past on their way to the door. The whole group seemed subdued, listless. I didn't get much more than a glance from any of them. No one spoke. What had happened down there while I was fighting goatheads outside?

Ashton wasn't behind them. I grabbed one of the students, a girl named Liz, gently by the arm and asked where he was.

119

She looked at me blankly for a second. "He's still downstairs," she said, then pulled her arm away and continued toward the front door.

I paused at the top of the stairs leading down into the vault. The sense of malevolence coming from that darkened opening was stronger than ever, as if whatever was down there was well aware of my efforts after I'd left, and hated me all the more for it. Going down there was going into the lion's den.

I touched the grip of my pistol, then the silver crucifix at my throat. That was when I realized that it was still hanging outside my shirt. That might have accounted for a few of the odder looks I'd gotten from the other students who had just left. I tucked it back inside. I wasn't ashamed of it; but I wanted to be able to engage Ashton without putting him on the defensive immediately, and the presence of such a symbol might do that. Especially given what might be whispering in his ear...

Taking another deep breath, I started down the stairs.

The blackness enclosed me almost immediately. It seemed thicker, almost tangible now. Looking back, I could see the door, but it seemed like light from the basement wasn't making it past the threshold. I could barely see my hand in front of my face. When I pulled out my light, it illuminated what it was pointed at, but not much else. I had to point it at my feet to see the steps I was reaching for.

I worked my way downward like that, halfway feeling my way like a blind man. Even the flickering candlelight from Ashton's little work area, while visible from around the corner, didn't seem to cast any usable light on the steps.

When I came out onto the floor of the vault, I could finally see. Ashton was standing at the bone table, leaning on it with both hands, studying the five objects he had spread out on the tabletop. Most of the candles had burned low, and smoke was curling up from one that had just gone out.

He didn't seem to notice me at first. He didn't even look up until I was less than six feet away. When he did, there was a new fire in his eyes, a look of triumph. I got that sinking feeling in my gut. He obviously thought he'd found what he was looking for. That was going to make talking him out of this foolishness even harder.

"Jed!" he said excitedly. At first it seemed like his old enthusiasm was back, but there was an edge to his excitement that hadn't been there before. When I got closer, I saw the same burning look in his eyes that had been there before I'd left. The excited academic was well and truly gone, replaced by the would-be sorcerer. "You came back. Good. I was upset when you left in the first place, but I realized that you're just the kind of guy who had to make sure the kids who weren't ready got home safe. Nothing wrong with that. But you came back. We can start getting ready for the next step."

I took another step toward him. "You have no idea what happened upstairs last night, do you?" I asked.

He frowned, looking momentarily distracted. It was like I'd suddenly derailed his train of thought, and he was lost for a moment. "What?"

"You didn't hear any of that?" I asked. I already knew the answer, but maybe confronting him with it would help. "You didn't hear the yelling and the shooting upstairs?"

Now he looked really lost. The fire in his eyes faded for a moment, and he looked a little scared. "Shooting? There was shooting? What happened?"

I told him, briefly but with detail. He looked completely bewildered at the description of the goatheads. I'd seen enough duplicity in him before that I couldn't be entirely sure how genuine his confusion was. But he seemed genuinely to have never heard of or seen any such creature. "You're sure you haven't seen anything like that around here?" I asked.

He shook his head. "I'm pretty sure I'd remember a goat-man," he said.

"What about a homunculus?" I asked.

That hit home. It was little more than a flicker across his face, but he definitely reacted to that. He knew something about that thing; not that I needed his reaction to tell. The smell of it in the house earlier had been all the confirmation I needed. He looked scared and trapped for a split second, but then the mask descended and he was in control again. "What do you know about homunculi?" he asked.

I shrugged. "Not much. I read a couple of books a while back that talked about them. Small, artificial men made of clay, herbs, and blood, and animated by magic. They usually have

121

disproportionately large heads. The thing I saw on the street last night was short and had a huge head. I've never heard of anything else like that, so I figured that must be what it was."

He looked startled at that, glancing at me sharply, as hard as he was working to keep his expression composed. Behind the mask, though, I could tell that something about what I'd just said made him deeply worried. Did that mean that he'd had no idea that the homunculus was out and about that night? It was yet another indication, to me, that this thing was getting out of his control, if he'd ever been in control of any of it in the first place. Still, he was so compartmentalized that I couldn't be sure of anything yet.

"Homunculi are fascinating," he said, as he turned his attention back to the books and artifacts in front of him. "A lot of people have tried to make them work, without success. They've been the holy grail of many people interested in the occult for a long time; the actual construction is fairly straightforward, but the animation is where things get difficult." He looked at me with that same fire, though there was a faint flicker of doubt behind his gaze, as if he suddenly didn't know what all was going on. "I actually built one, you know. I never showed it to anyone; for the longest time I thought it was going to be a failure. But the tablet showed me how to make it wake." He laid his hand on the Kozheozersky tablet again, staring down at it. "I experimented with it for a little while, but then the tablet started to show me so much more..." He waved at the table's contents. "This is...so far beyond homunculi that it boggles the mind."

He didn't wait for me to ask about the homunculus or why it had been following me. He launched right in. "This is going to open the door, Jed," he said, that obsessive fire back in his eyes, and a low, creepy intensity to his voice. "It's going to change everything." He looked back up at me. "As you know from the other night, I believe there's a chthonic spirit beneath Powell Hill. A genius loci, if you will. I don't know what all it knows, but what research I've been able to conduct suggest that its knowledge goes back to the earliest shamans who tested the boundaries of this world and the Otherworld in this area. They were before the Native Americans, before anyone else. Another people, from an earlier era we've never heard of.

"If we can contact this spirit, finally, it will open up secrets that we haven't even dreamed existed. But contacting it directly is difficult. From what I've discovered, it was bound beneath the hill at some point. I don't know exactly how, but these books and artifacts may well hold the key to undoing the binding. Then we can talk to the chthonic spirit, and then...then the things we will learn..." He kind of trailed off, still staring at the fan of objects on top of the bone table, lost in his dreams and seemingly oblivious to my presence.

The sense of impending doom had never been stronger. Somehow I knew that if he accomplished his aims, the results would be far worse than I could imagine. "You know," I ventured, "this is really some very dangerous stuff..."

His head snapped up and he stared at me, his eyes wide and bright. "Of course it is," he replied. "It's dangerous to the uninitiated, the foolish who do not treat it with respect. But we've studied, and we are willing to take the risks that come with the search for deep knowledge." I noticed the phrase "deep knowledge" immediately. It sounded strange, stranger than the words themselves might have suggested.

"No, it's dangerous to *anyone*," I told him, trying to talk him down off the ledge. "The last time I left here, that homunculus followed me. It *murdered* people, Clark. It tore their guts out and painted the walls with them. And they were occultists, just like you. You can't control this stuff."

Once again, that flicker of doubt and fear crossed his face as I mentioned the homunculus' killings. It was as if he hadn't known it was happening, and now that he did, he didn't know why, and it scared him. But then the arrogance and fevered intensity snapped into place again. "They were *not* just like me," he said hotly. "I know what I've gotten into. I know how to proceed, especially now that I've found these." He scowled at me. "Don't tell me you're getting scared, Jed? You faced an ifrit and lived to tell about it! Not one man in a million can say that. You have to have some kind of role to play, the Great Ones have to have had their eye on you, even then."

"'Great Ones?'" I interrupted. "The goatheads used that name, too. Who are the 'Great Ones?'"

"Don't you know yet?" he said. "You've been searching long enough. They are the powers of the earth, the ancient spirits

123

and forces of nature, the fae, the chthonic spirits, the old gods. Our own fears and superstitions divorced us from them, but the secrets of how to speak to them again are here to be found. And when we find them, and re-connect with them, we will become as gods ourselves."

I'd heard that line before. It never boded well. I resisted the urge to take a step back. His gaze was as intent and fevered as a madman's. He tilted his head as he looked at me, a not-entirely-human looking gesture. "You're not having second thoughts about this, are you, Jed?" he asked, his voice gone eerily calm. "That really wouldn't be a good idea. You've come far; turning back because of the superstitious fears of Christianity could have...consequences." He looked back down at the objects in front of him. "The Great Ones make demands of us, if we will have congress with them. Sometimes those demands are harsh. We have to accept our place in the cosmos if we are going to have a chance at being raised to a higher one, and sometimes that means sacrifices have to be made."

He stared at me again. "Some of those sacrifices are physical. Some are more...intangible." I took his meaning without elaboration. You'd only have to sacrifice your soul to these things for power or knowledge. Oldest line in the book. Faust would have been proud. "But one thing's for certain; once you start on the path, start to learn about them, they don't take kindly to rejection. They will have what they are owed; there is no escape to the Church or the Cross."

I'd heard enough. The time for subtlety was over. "I guess I'm just going to have to take my chances, then," I said. "I've seen enough." I didn't turn my back on him, or the blackness behind him, as I started moving back toward the steps.

A new whispering started in the dark. Low and ugly, it was like the whispering in the Drop Inn, only worse, if that was possible. The candles seemed to flicker even lower, and the darkness pressed in like a living thing. Ashton stayed where he was, staring at me with a mix of anger and what I can only describe as industrial-strength crazy on his face.

Having already thrown discretion to the winds, I drew my Colt and kept it at my side as I backed to the stairs. Shapes started to resolve in the shadows behind Ashton. None came closer, but the menace was tangible. "I thought you were special,

Jed," Ashton called, his voice just below a shout. "You survived meeting the ifrit! You were a fellow searcher! We could have been great—partners! We could have shared the power that the Great Ones could bestow on us!"

"You can still end this, Clark," I told him, trying one last time. "You can still walk away."

I could never be sure, then or after, if what I saw next was real or simply an impression brought on by the whispering and the barely-visible shapes in the darkness. But it looked like a pair of long-fingered, shadowy hands settled on Ashton's shoulders. It might have just been a trick of the dying candlelight, but it almost seemed as if fear flitted across his face just before he said, "No, I can't. And you'll regret walking away, yourself."

I was at the stairs. I wasn't ready for whatever confrontation was going to happen here, not yet. So I turned and ran. I sprinted up the steps, even as Ashton let out a strangled, inarticulate yell of anger and frustration.

The stairs were longer than I remembered, and that wasn't just the fear making it seem that way. By the time I reached the top I was smoked, my legs burning and my chest heaving. I'd just run up what must have been fifty steps or more. I had no idea how that was possible, but it had happened, somehow. Apparently, one of Ashton's "powers of the earth" was at work.

I didn't slow down until I was out of the house. As I scooped up the backpack with the torch in it, I looked back up at the house. It looked darker, even in the increasingly clear and bright light of day, almost as if the house was under a thundercloud. Nothing had really changed, structurally, but the house lay under a cloud of almost tangible evil now. The windows had become black, soulless eyes staring at the world with undisguised malevolence. If it had suddenly turned into Dracula's castle, it couldn't have looked more sinister.

Dan was already waiting for me out front, the Bronco's engine running. I got in as quick as I could get out of the gate, my Colt still in my hand. I shoved the backpack into the leg space in front of the seat as I slammed the door.

"Well, no going in through the front door anymore," I said. "That way's closed."

"He didn't take the come-to-Jesus talk well, did he?" Dan asked as he pulled us away from the curb.

I shook my head. "No, he didn't. And I don't think his 'sponsors' did, either." I glanced back over my shoulder, but the house was already obscured by the surrounding trees and hedges. It didn't matter; the sense of malicious watchfulness was still there.

"So what do we do now?" I asked.

Dan glanced at me. "You've got a better picture of the situation up-close than I do," he said. "What do you think we should do?"

That brought me up short. I was a newbie; I didn't know what to do. Dan was the expert. He was supposed to tell me what to do.

"Listen, kid," Dan said, "there simply aren't enough of us to have somebody holding your hand long enough to learn everything. There comes a time where you've got to sink or swim, trust in God and go with what you think will work. The sooner you get the hang of that, the better."

I stared out the windshield and frowned, thinking. What he said made sense, and wasn't all that different from what a few of my small-unit leaders had done in the Marine Corps. You can't always have somebody there to guide you along, so you get put in a position where you've got to make a decision and stick with it, while there's still somebody there to catch you if you start sinking.

"He knows that I'm not on his side now," I said after a long moment. "I'm pretty sure that whatever's pulling his strings has known for a while now."

"So you're certain there's another direct influence?" Dan asked. "He's not just groping?"

I shook my head. "Someone or something is steering him. Subtly, but it's definitely happening. I think he may have started out on his own, but whatever it is started taking the reins a while ago. He didn't know the homunculus was out and about last night, and he was preoccupied enough with the research down in the vault that he couldn't have been controlling it anyway. And I'm fairly sure there was something downstairs with him in the dark, just now." I told him about the impression of darkened hands on Ashton's shoulders, and the lengthened stairs.

"That's not good," Dan said. "That would mean that something is already reaching out of the Abyss, if it hasn't already come through." He rubbed his face tiredly. It just reminded me of how bone-weary I was after being up all night, facing the horrors that had come out of the dark. "Any idea what he's planning?"

"He wants to try to contact whatever's up by Powell Hill again. He thinks it'll be the key to his 'deep knowledge' or whatever," I replied.

Dan frowned. "'Deep knowledge?' Did he say that?"

"He did." I studied him curiously. "It caught my attention, too, like it's somehow significant. Any idea why?"

He shook his head, still frowning. It took a while before he finally answered. "No, I don't actually know...strange. For a moment it seemed like I should, but I've got nothing. Huh."

Something about that disturbed me, almost as much as the sense of oppressive malice hovering around that house. "That doesn't seem right to me," I said. "Why should that phrase make both of us think it means something, but neither of us can say how?"

"We'll ask Father Ignacio later," he said. "What's your plan for today?"

I thought about it. "There's something down in that vault," I said. "Something that's somehow influencing what's going on. Maybe it's the tablet, but I think the best thing to do is going to be getting into that vault and smashing whatever paraphernalia he's got that can help him conduct the ritual, preferably before sundown."

"But you said the front door is out," Dan pointed out.

I grimaced. "At least if we're going to try to be discreet about it, it is," I said. "But unless there's another way in, we may have to kick in the door and deal with the consequences afterward."

"Hmm." Dan frowned thoughtfully out the windshield for a moment. "There may be another way. Let's go track down Ari. I'm pretty sure he hasn't left town yet, and there are still things he can do besides fight monsters."

Chapter 11

After a long, roundabout drive away from the house, we came back to the church. Father Ignacio's bike was still parked out front, and there were still .45-70 and .50 Beowulf casings littering the steps. There was no sign of the goatheads or anything else uncanny, though. That had all vanished with the sunrise.

There were a few new people gathered outside the church; they looked like some of the neighbors, mostly students at Howard Phillips. Dan parked about a half a block from the church, and we studied the small crowd on the church steps.

The front door was slightly ajar, and there was a figure standing in it; Father Ignacio was immediately recognizable, his Roman collar standing out against his biker leathers. He was talking to the group, everybody appeared reasonably calm, and nobody appeared to be calling the cops. So far, so good.

"Better leave the rifles in the truck," Dan said, echoing my own thoughts on the matter. As calm as everybody looked, in spite of the fact that they were standing in our expended brass from the night before, there was no point in tempting fate. The last thing we needed was somebody calling the cops at this point. If somebody wanted to call the cops after we'd stopped Ashton, fine. We'd deal with that when we came to it. But getting rolled up for shooting in town could be disastrous, especially if Ashton was aiming at awakening the thing at Powell Hill that night.

Something was still bothering me about that. It was just like the reaction to the "deep knowledge" phrase; some niggling thought just at the edge of consciousness. A doubt that wouldn't fully take shape.

We got out and approached the steps. The crowd was muttering, but there didn't seem to be any overt hostility, just confusion. "What's going on?" I asked, deciding to go ahead and engage first.

Several of the younger people on the edge of the small crowd turned to look at us. One, a burly, football-player type, answered. "Something happened here last night," he said. "There were a lot of weird noises and some shooting. Nobody could get through to the cops, either; even cell phones weren't working. We just came to see what had happened."

"I'm telling you, I saw what I saw," a skinny, sharp-featured guy was saying. The woman next to him looked skeptical. "There was a crowd around the church, chanting something."

So, someone *had* seen what had gone down. And apparently, something had blocked any communications, which explained why the cops hadn't come when Dan and I started shooting.

"Why would anyone do that?" I asked, playing the innocent. I wasn't really expecting a serious answer, but what I got kind of surprised me.

"There's a history of that kind of thing around here," the skinny kid insisted. "It goes back quite a long time, too."

"Oh, come on, George," the woman next to the skinny guy said. "Nobody believes that conspiracy crap."

"It's *not* a conspiracy theory," George retorted. "It's history; recorded fact."

"Whatever," the woman said, and turned away. "Somebody was being rowdy last night, that's all. It doesn't look like anybody got hurt, or like anything was damaged, so let's just go."

The crowd was starting to break up, and Father Ignacio wasn't disputing the woman's assertion. George looked frustrated, and looked like he was going to linger. I glanced over at Dan and tilted my head fractionally toward George. He nodded just as subtly, and I moved toward the younger man. Maybe he knew something that might help.

"George, is it?" I asked, as soon as I was sure no one was really paying attention. "You know something about this sort of thing?"

He looked at me sharply, with the sort of distrust you see from someone expecting to be mocked as soon as he opens his mouth. I kept my face carefully composed; I didn't want to look too eager, but I sure didn't want him to think I didn't believe him. After all, I was pretty sure that *something* had happened around here before, just judging by the presence of the vault. Ashton sure hadn't excavated that thing himself.

"Yeah, I do," he said, with a bit of a combative edge to his voice. "I've been studying local history quite a bit. There are some odd things about it, but nobody wants to hear about them. They challenge people's complacency."

"We'd be interested to hear about it," I said. "You mind sitting down with us for a bit?"

He looked back and forth between me and Dan, as if trying to gauge if we were serious, or just trying to yank his chain. He frowned, but finally said, "Yeah, I'll give you a rundown about it. But not here. I start talking and people start disbelieving. You want to talk, we go to my office, and I can show you all the evidence before you start asking questions."

I confess, my eyebrows went up at that. "Yeah, my office," he said defensively. "Well, I call it my office, and it may as well be. I've got all my supporting evidence gathered there; photos, newspaper clippings, recordings of interviews, the whole nine yards. Come on."

I glanced over at Dan and frowned a little. This guy was awfully eager to show us everything. But given the time crunch we were probably under, I wasn't going to look a gift horse in the mouth. If he could provide some insight on not only the occult history of the town, but possibly of the house and the vault themselves, that could be a big help.

Of course, he could also just be a crackpot, in which case we were wasting valuable time.

He quickly agreed to ride in Dan's truck. I didn't see any car that looked like it belonged to him; most of the cars on the

130

street were disappearing as the crowd drove away. I got the rifles wrapped in cloths and shoved under the back seat before we let him in. He may have been all right, but I wasn't interested in taking any more chances than necessary at that point.

His directions to his place were short and clear, and we were there in a matter of minutes. His "office" was a one-room studio apartment, that was also apparently his living quarters. The walls were almost invisible behind piles of books and newspapers. The parts that weren't were covered in small cork bulletin-boards with more newspaper clippings tacked to them. Several notebooks were opened with various scribbled notes, scattered on the tiny computer desk, the floor, and the bed. A small, ancient-looking laptop was open on the desk.

He went to a binder first. When he opened it up, it was full of neatly organized, very old newspaper clippings. "The beginning wasn't actually all that long ago," he began, handing over the binder. "The town hasn't been here long enough. But in 1901, a small group of occultists started their own little secret society here, called the Society of Illuminated Inquirers. I know, I know" he said, when we looked skeptical, "it's pretentious as hell. It kind of fits turn-of-the-century occultists, though." Dan nodded at that. I didn't know enough about such things to have an opinion one way or another.

He flipped through several pages. "They were sort of a local curiosity for a while. There were a few local puff pieces written about them. What's more interesting is what *wasn't* written about them."

He came to the page he was looking for and pointed to a series of obituaries. "In the course of three weeks, there were fifteen unexplained deaths, all of girls between the ages of fifteen and seventeen. Eventually, a man named Logan Everett was arrested and charged with murdering ten of them. He was found guilty and hanged.

"Case closed, right? Well, he protested his innocence up until the trap door opened under his feet. I know, they all do that. But here's the thing; none of the girls' bodies were ever found, and shortly after the disappearances stopped, the Society of Illuminated Inquirers purchased the land where the Feist House stands today.

"They were the ones who built the house. Did you know there's a vault beneath it?"

I nodded. "Yeah, we know."

He seemed a little taken aback at that. Apparently, most people he gave this little presentation to either weren't interested enough, or were simply ignorant of what he was talking about. He of course had no idea why we were interested, but he seemed like one of those guys who was just so excited that somebody would listen to him that he didn't care.

"Well, the vault was a later addition," he said, once he got back on his mental track. "The original Society stuck with just the house." He shuffled around until he dragged up a couple more notebooks. "There weren't any more sprees of disappearances, but they did happen every once in a while. Some of the locals—and this got passed down to grandchildren mostly, though I was able to interview one old lady who was a child at the time—reported all sorts of strange sounds around the house, usually within a few days of the disappearances."

"Nobody ever investigated?" I asked.

He shook his head. "Not that I can find. The papers never mentioned anything of the sort, either. Which tells me one thing; the Society had its fingers pretty deep in the rest of the town."

Dan nodded. "Small towns can sometimes get that way," he said. "I've been in more than one where what the papers *didn't* say was even more informative than what they did."

"It also explains how they were able to continue to grow bigger here," George continued. "Based on some of the ledgers I've found in my research, and some private letters that made their way, somehow, into the local library, by the 1930s the Society essentially owned the town." He flipped through another binder, this one with what looked like photocopies of handwritten letters on the pages. "It never said so specifically anywhere else, but there were enough people who thought that the Society approved candidates for Mayor and Chief of Police. Most of these people were later forced out of town somehow, usually by accusations of dishonest business practices, though Adam Shield, here--" he indicated a particular letter "--must have been getting a little too close. He was accused of molesting his nephew; he was never actually charged, but the accusation was enough to drive him out of town. He was pretty specific in his letters as to who was getting paid by whom."

He kept pulling documents out of stacks of binders, even less-organized stacks of papers, and shoeboxes piled on the floor. He'd been at this for quite a while.

"Are you writing a book?" I asked suddenly.

He chuckled. "It didn't start that way. It was just going to be a paper for a psychology course. It...kinda ballooned a little."

I looked around at the piles of research material. "I'll say," I replied.

"In the early '30s," George said, as he found whatever he was looking for and spread it on the table, "the local parish priest, a Father Vincent Schmidt, tried to take a stand against the Society. The papers and the letters paint very different pictures of what was going on in the town at that point. The papers made it out to be almost Norman Rockwell's America. The locals, those who weren't impressed with the Society at least, described crimes that didn't get reported, corruption, plenty of sexual assaults, even some cases of what I can only describe as slavery. And all of it seemed to be run out of that house.

"Father Schmidt's stand became a rallying cry for anyone disaffected with the town's consensus. The result was ugly.

"The priest and his allies weren't even being that confrontational. It hadn't gotten to that point yet. They were just meeting regularly—almost nightly, judging by some of the letters I've found—to try to discuss just *what* to do. It sounded like a lot of them were ready to just pull stakes and move away. There's a lot of near-despair in what I've found.

"At any rate, on the night of October 31, 1937, the church burned down. It wasn't where the new one is, either; it was closer to the center of town. The papers said it was an accidental fire caused when a votive candle was knocked over. The eyewitnesses say something different." He pointed to an old reel-to-reel tape recorder in the corner. "According to an interview with Jacob Dodson, one of Father Schmidt's parishioners, in 1956, there was a crowd gathered outside the church before it burned, chanting something. He said he couldn't tell exactly what they were chanting, but that it was disturbing. He said that the church was attacked, and that the crowd burned it down, along

133

with all of the parishioners that the papers reported 'died from smoke inhalation.'"

"So you're saying that the last resistance to this 'Society' was wiped out in the late '30s?" I asked. "And this 'Society' is running the town now?"

He shook his head. "I don't think it is, no," he replied. "I'm still working on finding out exactly what happened, but the Society lost a lot of ground in the '50s. That was when Dodson finally felt he could come out with his story of what had happened in 1937. By the time the '60s rolled around, there's no trace of the Society left at all. In fact, some of the fates of its members are as mysterious as the disappearances here at the turn of the century.

"But even though the Society seems to be gone, there's still been a lot of weird stuff happening around that house ever since. In the late '70s, Spiro Damien, the occultist, moved in and had the vault built."

Now he had my attention. I was starting to think that this was going to turn into a bit of historical curiosity and nothing more. If he knew more about the vault, though...

"He never confided in anyone what he was building it for, but the plans were duly filed with the city manager's office. I was able to get them." After a bunch of rummaging, he pulled a rumpled handful of papers out of yet another pile, looked around for a second, and spread them on the bed. "It was very carefully laid out, with thirteen pillars inside and an inlaid circle of symbols in the center of the floor." He looked up at us. "There are stories that the workers who put the circle in went crazy and had to be institutionalized, but I haven't found any supporting evidence that anything like that actually happened."

I was studying the plans. The vault was quite a bit bigger than I'd been able to see. That was really no surprise; what was a surprise was just *how much* bigger it really was. It was about twice the size of the house itself, and the house wasn't exactly small. It also looked like there were more entrances. "Are there more ways in than the stairs from the house?" I asked, wanting to make sure that that was what I was looking at.

"There are eight," he confirmed. "That was part of Damien's specific plan. There are eight tunnels branching out from the central vault, in the rough shape of the 'chaos star' that first started showing up in occult circles in the '70s." He hesitated, as if uncertain whether or not he should say anything more. "Some people who have been in the tunnels have said that they change length," he said finally. "Almost as if either the tunnels or the vault aren't staying in one place. It's ridiculous, I know, but it's just one of the stories about the place, and kind of shows how weird it is."

I just raised an eyebrow and said nothing. It suddenly sounded like there was more to what had happened on my retreat from the vault than just fear making the stairs seem longer. I also thought I saw a useful bit of information. "Are the entrances to the tunnels recorded?" I asked.

He nodded, and pulled up a map. It had several marks and notes scribbled on it. "They don't quite fit the straight-line mapping, but they are there. I've been able to actually find one; I'm pretty sure that several of them aren't accessible anymore. One at least has a new house on top of it." I wondered how that was working out for the house's occupants. "That place, interestingly enough," he continued, "has seen six different owners in just the last two years." I guess that answered that question.

"Which one would be the easiest to access?" Dan asked, beating me to the punch. "Do you know?"

George didn't hesitate. He pointed to one in a park a couple of blocks away from the house. "This one. It's back in the trees; nobody's likely to see you going into it unless they're watching it. It's also the only one that I know for certain is still accessible, too." He looked at us both intently. "You guys think there's still something going on there, don't you?" he asked.

"We know there is," Dan said grimly. "And we're going to do something to stop it."

It took some time to find the entrance, even with George's instructions. Damien had apparently been worried about somebody discovering his little underground occult lair. Finally, my boot made a hollow thumping sound that didn't fit right. Some digging around revealed a cleverly disguised trap door set into the roots of a sycamore that looked like it had been growing there for almost a century.

It wasn't locked, but it was heavy and fitted tightly into its frame. There were also a number of symbols carved into it, which made me uneasy until Father Ignacio blessed them carefully.

Even after who knows how long without being opened, the trap door swung open without much more noise than the rasp of wood on wood. There was no squeaking of rusty hinges, and it didn't take a huge amount of muscle power to get it up. It swung open to rest flat on the ground, leaving an opening about three feet across leading down into the dark.

I pointed my flashlight down into the hole. There was a metal ladder leading down, against the tree-trunk side of the shaft. It had been painted, and while there were a few scuffs in the paint on the rungs, it was pretty well preserved. The sides had been covered in planks, which were showing a few signs of mold and rot. One had been forced out from the wall by an intruding tree root.

There was nothing else. The shaft looked about twenty feet deep. No traps, no adornment, nothing but the ladder and the shaft. I looked up at Dan and Father Ignacio. "Well, I guess there's nothing for it," I said. Putting my light between my teeth, I swung my legs down into the hole, feeling for the rungs of the ladder. Once my boots were solidly on the first rung, I started down. Above me, I could hear Father Ignacio begin his litany. He was calling on the Saints to pray for us, the Angels to fight by our sides, and the Power of God to watch over and protect us, and chastise the powers of the Abyss.

While the walls had been planked, essentially making the shaft a long, narrow box buried in the earth, the bottom was packed dirt and gravel. It was wet, and the bottom of the planking was definitely starting to rot away. The very bottom rung of the ladder was sagging as the wood it was set into went mushy. I guess Damien hadn't thought to use treated lumber.

The entrance to the tunnel was behind me as I got to the base of the ladder. I felt it before I really saw it. It was like the feeling you get when somebody's staring at the back of your head. You don't know why you feel it, but you do. The fairly narrow, short doorway built into the side of the shaft was transformed by my own dread into a gaping maw, waiting to swallow all three of us.

I stepped into the tunnel, ducking my head to avoid the ceiling. We wouldn't have to crawl, but it still wasn't going to be comfortable; it wouldn't have been even if there wasn't some sort of soul-devouring evil waiting at the other end. Father Ignacio started down the ladder as soon as it was clear.

My light showed the tunnel had been braced with timbers, but otherwise was packed earth and rocks. Roots came out of the ceiling and walls, but never protruded very far. I would have expected more overgrowth, since the tunnel had apparently been there since the '70s, but it was fairly clear. Whether that meant someone was tending it or what, I didn't know.

I drew my Colt, keeping my light in my off hand, and started down the tunnel. Father Ignacio was close behind me, and Dan would take up the rear. There was no point in prolonging the agony by hanging out in the tunnel, waiting for whatever might come up out of the dark at our intrusion. We were committed, so we may as well press forward.

It was very quiet down there. My footfalls, even as light as I made them, crunched loudly on the wet loam and gravel of the floor. I had to fight not to flinch with every sound. The silence seemed almost...watchful. As if something was down there, holding its breath, waiting for us. Father Ignacio's murmured prayer sounded like a roar. With every step, I expected a pack of goatheads to materialize out of the darkness ahead, charging us in the cramped quarters of the tunnel.

But still nothing appeared. It was cold, damp, and oppressively silent, aside from our footfalls.

After several minutes, that felt like even longer, it was becoming apparent to me that the tunnel was doing the same strange "stretching" thing that the stairs had done earlier, when I'd retreated from the vault. I was sure we had to have come far enough to have reached the vault.

I stopped suddenly, raising my hand, and Dan and Father Ignacio froze behind me. I kept my light on, but didn't move, and barely breathed. I'd thought I'd heard something.

At first, it was just silent, so quiet that it was almost like the silence was deafeningly loud, if that makes any sense. Then I started to hear it. Whispering.

The sound was just barely above the threshold of my hearing, and I couldn't make out any words. It was just barely there, an unintelligible susurration that just kind of oozed menace from the very walls. I started walking again, if only to start making a little noise and hopefully drown out the sound of the whispering. I was pretty sure I didn't want to be able to make out the words. Father increased the volume of his litany.

But even driving on and making some noise didn't make the whispers go away. They stayed, just below the threshold of understanding, like an itch I couldn't scratch. They seemed to stay just loud enough to be audible in spite of Father Ignacio's prayers. I forced myself to ignore them and continue moving forward.

Finally, the tunnel came to an end. At first it looked like it was a dead end; the passage ended with a brick wall. But as I came closer and examined it, the brick wall was actually a carefully disguised door. A good push and it swung away from me, with a faint grinding noise. Even that didn't drown out the whispers. It was like whatever noise we made, the whispering was always going to be there, just barely loud enough to hear. It was starting to irritate me, to be honest.

The door opened on pitch blackness. As I stepped through, though, quickly moving aside to clear the way for Father Ignacio and Dan, I was certain it was the vault. I could feel it.

I swept my light around the open space. It was huge, much larger than the part we'd seen by candlelight with Ashton the night before. The pillars were unevenly spaced around the room, and carved with various twisted, ugly creatures that I didn't want to examine too closely.

The jumble of cases, chests, stacks, and tables where we had been examining the various texts and artifacts with Ashton sat across the vault from our point of entry. What the dim light and darkness had disguised was the fact that the collection didn't extend much farther than we'd been able to see. Most of the rest of the vault was open space. So much for Ashton's assurance that the vault was "packed" with artifacts.

It wasn't empty, though. There were statues against the walls, and another, larger one dominating the space opposite the stairs, where it had faced us the entire night, back in the dark where we couldn't see it. It was a vile image, a leering face crowned with four horns and sitting atop a bloated, misshapen body sprouting an uneven number of twisted, deformed limbs.

While it faced the stairs, which were almost halfway around the vault from us, it still seemed to be staring at us.

The rest of the statues were almost as grotesque as the big one. As I continued to sweep my light across the room, illuminating the dull gleam of the demonic symbols inlaid in the floor, it shone on a short, pale figure standing on top of the circle of glyphs, facing us, staring with dull, black button eyes and a vacant, idiot grin. The sour, stale-vomit smell hit my nostrils like a brick.

The homunculus was waiting for us.

Chapter 12

Dan had turned on his own light as he cleared my back, and it now focused on the homunculus as well. Somehow, the thing seemed to be staring at both of us, even as we spread out to cover it from a couple of different directions. Father Ignacio had brought his own intensely bright light, which he added to our own as soon as he came through the door. He may not have been packing heat like Dan and I were, but I wouldn't discount him in a fight with this thing. He hadn't stopped reciting that litany; he now increased its volume, his gravelly voice rolling across the vault.

My pistol wasn't the only weapon I'd brought, either. There was a little present for the homunculus in the pack on my back. I just had to get it out without getting my head ripped off.

I was trying to watch the homunculus and keep an eye out for anything else that might be lurking in the dark. None of the goatheads had appeared, but I was expecting some sort of unpleasant surprise at any moment. Not that the homunculus didn't count as such.

When I glanced back at it, its mouth opened. At first there was a scratching sort of screech from it, like feedback from a microphone. Then it started talking.

140

At least, it was attempting to talk. What came out was little more than mumbling, in a sort of distant, distorted tone like a weak radio signal. There was a scratchy sort of interference in the sound, further reinforcing the impression of a sort of remote-controlled monster.

The fact that it was speaking complete mumbling gibberish didn't make it any less disturbing. In a way, it made it worse, especially as its volume kept going up and down, as if it was trying to emphasize certain things, even though what it was saying made no sense. A couple of times, its noise ascended to a blast of sound that echoed painfully through the vault. Its mouth was moving as it talked, though it was completely out of sync with the sounds coming out.

The grotesque thing hadn't moved at all. It just stood there, staring, yelling its incoherent gibberish. At least, it didn't look like it moved. Yet somehow it always seemed to be facing me when I looked at it. I wondered if Dan was seeing the same thing.

Long habit kept screaming at me to look around, to check my back even as the homunculus screamed and gibbered, but to do that would have meant taking my eyes and light off the homunculus, and something told me that would be a bad idea. Frankly, I'm not sure why, but I somehow felt like if I turned my back on it, it would come after me, and I wouldn't be able to react in time.

Unfortunately, the only thing I had with me that I was fairly certain had a chance of destroying that thing was on my back. I'd have to put my light or my pistol down to get to it.

"Dan," I called, "I'm going to need you to cover me."

"Do what you've got to do," he replied, from off to my right. "I've got you."

I had to decide which to lower first; pistol or light. I didn't exactly trust that the light was blinding the homunculus...who knew if that thing saw like we did in the first place?

Finally, I decided I just had to trust that Dan could keep it off me while I pulled out my little surprise.

I started to lower the pistol, banking on the light to hopefully keep it from seeing the gun muzzle come off of it, when

141

suddenly the homunculus went silent. When it spoke again, it was suddenly understandable.

"Jedediah," it creaked, still sounding like an interference-laced broadcast on an old, vacuum-tube radio, the volume increasing as it tried to shout down Father Ignacio's prayers. "Why do you still try to fight the Great Ones' purpose? Do you think that you can somehow rise above what you have done? That you can somehow become 'purified' of your congress with us? If so, you are a fool. You have been among us, you have sought the old knowledge that only the Great Ones are willing to share. You have tasted the fruit, and now you are tainted with the rest. The Enemy will turn his face from you, no matter what you do here."

Its voice was changing volume and tone randomly, like a signal fading in and out. "You belong to the Great Ones," it continued. "Why, then, continue to anger them? If you turn back and devote yourself to them now, perhaps their wrath will not be as terrible when you face them again. Sacrifice these two to them, and save yourself."

"Hey!" Father Ignacio shouted. I could see him shining his own flashlight on that big silver crucifix of his. "Shut it!"

The homunculus actually flinched, the first real movement I'd seen out of it since we'd come down into the vault. It's mouth gaped a little wider, and it went back to spouting feedback-laced gibberish.

"Jed?" Dan called, "You good?"

"I'm good," I assured him. "If that was the best it had, it was pretty weak."

I probably shouldn't have said that. With an ear-splitting, crackling shriek, it rushed at me. It was surprisingly fast for the jerky, marionette sort of way it moved. It was on me in an eyeblink, and swatted me with one hand. I went sprawling, my flashlight spinning out of my hand and almost losing my grip on my pistol. The light stayed on as it spun away, bright white light flickering across the vault, lending a further sureality to the scene.

The homunculus was right on top of me as I slid to a halt, my head ringing from the impact. I got one shot off at it before it hit me again, a tooth-rattling, bone jarring slap that bounced my head off the stone floor. I saw stars. I didn't know where the gun was, at least until I heard the homunculus kick it away. It skittered across the floor, far out of my reach.

Now all I had was the crucifix around my neck, the knife at my belt, the flask of holy water in my hip pocket, and the backpack that was digging into my back, out of reach. There was no way to get to it unless I got this thing off me.

Unfortunately, that was going to be more easily said than done. I had both hands up in front of my head, trying to ward off the hammer blows it was raining down on me. That thing hit *hard*, harder than any man's ever hit me before. It was apparently still bound by Father Ignacio's command to shut up, as it didn't say anything, but kept howling that static-laden gibberish as it stood over me and battered my guard.

Thunder shattered the air. Flame spat from the muzzle of Dan's big hand-cannon, brilliant flashes that lit up the homunculus' grotesquely blank, waxy face. The shock of the muzzle blasts slapped me, but even the blast of a .44 magnum didn't seem as brutal as that thing's blows.

The bullets didn't do squat, which was no surprise. But when Father Ignacio advanced on it, shouting now, invoking the Saint Michael and the Holy Trinity and holding that big crucifix in front of him, it was forced back, cringing in front of the sacred image. I was able to scramble backward, away from it, still rattled by the beating it had given me in only a few short moments. I wasn't even that focused on trying to hurt it at first; I just wanted to get away from those club-like fists and the bottomless malice driving them.

I almost ran into Father Ignacio in my backwards, limping crawl. He was still shining that light on the homunculus, and holding up that gleaming crucifix, which seemed to shine even more brightly down there than it had outside the church the night before. The homunculus flinched away from the sight, the words of the prayer hitting it like physical blows, holding up its hands to shield its blank, black eyes.

It backed away from Father Ignacio, but it was still sidling its way around toward me. Father Ignacio moved to block it each time it tried to get around him, but it kept looking for an opening.

I started struggling to get the backpack off. Even through the fog of pain and horror in my battered brain, I still knew that the only physical means we had of possibly destroying this thing was on my back. The first strap didn't want to come off, though; my wrist was getting jammed up trying to pull it off.

Dan kept shooting, hammering the homunculus with heavy, silver-jacketed slugs, but all that was doing was sort of keeping it busy. Father Ignacio was doing more to keep it at bay, but it was only a matter of time before it found an opening. It was just too fast.

I had finally thrashed my arm clear of the first strap and was starting to sit up and swing the pack around when it found its opening. Disregarding the gunfire, it darted away from Father Ignacio, slammed into Dan, and came at me. I felt Dan's last shot smack into the ground only inches away from me, as the homunculus slapped his gun off-line before he could slacken his trigger finger. That did not help my already rattled nerves.

It was on me again in a heartbeat, picking me up off the floor. It hit me in the face with a hand that felt like a baseball bat, and then threw me about six feet. I smacked into one of the statues, feeling a stone appendage crack into my side, before falling to the floor. I was pretty sure I'd broken a rib or two.

Sure enough, when I sucked in a labored breath a sharp pain stabbed into my side. Definitely cracked, at least. I picked myself up, all too slowly, even as the homunculus was forced back again by Father Ignacio's crucifix. He was biting out the words of the long litany now, his voice loud, tight, and angry. They lashed the homunculus like nothing we'd been able to manage with gunfire.

As I stood up, I realized I'd lost the pack. I looked around frantically, but couldn't see where it had landed; it must have ended up in the shadows somewhere. I had to find it. But as I used the statue behind me to lever myself to my feet, the statue *moved*.

I don't mean it rocked or shifted, or anything explainable like that. No, that stony arm or tentacle or whatever it was that I'd gripped to pull myself up twisted around and grabbed my hand.

Its grip was hard and painful, stony talons digging into my arm and drawing blood. Just like before, I was having more trouble with the fog of pain and disorientation of having my body knocked around like a dog's chew toy than with the horror of

144

what was going on. Once again, I'd apparently hit the point where I couldn't get any more afraid, so I'd reached a sort of equilibrium.

Even as my knees buckled from the pain of the statue's vise-like grip, my mind was starting to clear. The homunculus was only a few feet away, still trying to find a way past Father Ignacio. I only had a couple weapons left, and I was pretty sure the knife wasn't going to help against the statue.

With my free hand, I dug the steel flask of holy water out of my back pocket. At first the cap didn't want to come loose. The lid had been screwed closed too tightly to be opened easily with one hand. Finally, after a couple seconds of fumbling, I put the cap in my teeth, twisted it open, and splashed some of the holy water liberally on the statue holding me in a rough sign of the Cross.

It released me instantly, with an ear-splitting scream of hate and anguish that almost drove me to my knees again. The stone actually *smoked* where the water had hit it, and the smell of scorched flesh and sulfur filled the air.

I scrambled away from the statue, almost falling on my face in my wounded haste. I had to find that pack.

Dan was shooting again, apparently unaware how close he'd come to blowing my head off, but since he'd repositioned himself to try to drive the homunculus away from me, I wasn't too worried about it. The bullets weren't doing much more than irritating the thing, but any little bit helped at that point. Father was doing the most to keep it at bay, but so far it was still kicking. That needed to change.

I finally spotted the pack in the spilled light from Dan's and Father Ignacio's flashlights. It was lying next to one of the pillars. Enough light shone on the pillar itself to show me more of what was carved on it than I cared to see, but I focused on getting to that pack.

The homunculus, or whatever was controlling it, seemed to realize that that pack contained its demise, and it tried to dart in to hit me again. Father Ignacio was ready for it, though, and kept diverting it to one side or another. It *really* couldn't take looking at that crucifix for more than a second or two, and it was slowing down, like the prayer was hurting it as badly as its blows had hurt me.

Half running, half crawling, I made it to the pack, ripped it open, and pulled out the butane torch and the hose of the little pump lawn sprayer we'd filled with gasoline. I pumped the sprayer frantically to get the pressure up with one hand, while I tried to get the torch lit with the other.

The sprayer only took a couple of pumps; I'd primed it before we had started out. The torch, though, didn't want to start. I clicked the igniter about four times before it finally caught. By then the homunculus was almost on me again. When it saw the little blue flame hiss into life, though, it stopped dead.

"Yeah, you don't like fire much, do you?" I croaked. I lifted the little sprayer and doused the thing in gasoline.

It tried to scramble backward, but it couldn't avoid the spray. It seemed almost a little disoriented, making weird, uneven mewling noises as I sprayed it down. Then I thrust the butane flame into the stream.

The gas ignited with a *whoosh*, and in an eyeblink the homunculus was engulfed in flame. It didn't stumble about in agony, but just stood there, blazing like a torch, letting out a long, distorted scream that didn't end until it was a waxy lump of burning stuff on the floor, no longer resembling anything remotely human.

Dan was at my side, helping me stand. "You all right, Jed?" he asked.

"Ow," was my only reply. I was pretty sure I'd be having a hard time moving for a couple of days at least. I staggered as I went to retrieve my pistol and flashlight, still looking around for the next surprise to come out of the dark. Getting grabbed by that statue had been a hell of a shock.

I dropped the magazine and op-checked the pistol when I picked it up. I was pretty sure the old piece would work fine, but after getting launched halfway across the vault, I wanted to be sure. It seemed alright, so I reloaded and joined Dan and Father Ignacio at the circle in the center of the room.

I would have thought, from its appearance, that the homunculus would have smelled like burning plastic or something when I set it on fire. The stench that filled the vault was closer to burned blood and something else, some elusive but disgusting stench that I couldn't quite identify. It reminded me of the trash-burning pits in Iraq. It stank.

146

The glyphs formed a twisted, interlocking web on the floor in front of the big idol. There was something more than a little disquieting about them. It's not something I can really describe; they were wrong on a sort of subconscious, primal level. Dan was already digging in his own pack for the hammer he'd brought, and Father Ignacio had a gallon of holy water.

"I'm going upstairs," I announced. "If Ashton's here, he will have noticed something going on down here. If not because of the noise, then I'm sure something from down here will have let him know."

Dan just nodded. "Makes sense. Are you good to go up on your own?"

I nodded, trying not to wince at the pain throbbing through every inch of my body. "I'll have to be," I replied. "I don't think we've got time to dilly-dally." I flexed my fingers around my Colt's grip. "I'll be all right."

Dan nodded, hefting the hammer. It was a short-handled, four-pound sledge. Dan was about to get his vandalism on. Father Ignacio's gallon of holy water was going to do most of the work, but defacing the symbols would help, too. I still had about half the tank in the sprayer full of gasoline, but I'd leave it downstairs for the moment.

The shelves, cases, and tables still had their candles, though they had all burned down to cold lumps of wax. The sense of menace among the artifacts was still there, though rather muted compared to what was back in the rest of the vault. This stuff was the shiny lure in front of the angler-fish's jaws.

I did notice, even as I made my stiff, painful way toward the stairs, that the tablet wasn't there, and neither were any of the books Ashton had been looking at. He'd already taken them upstairs, then.

I couldn't dash up the steps. Any jostling or really deep breaths made my ribs hurt like fire. Just like before, the surrounding shadows seemed to drink up all the light except where the flashlight beam hit directly.

The stairs didn't seem as long as the last time. Apparently the randomly varying geometries of the ways in and out of the vault were still in effect. It wasn't getting any less disturbing; tunnels and stairways aren't supposed to change like that, and even expecting it doesn't take away from that underlying sense of weirdness.

I paused at the door into the basement. It was just like breaching any door when I was still a Marine. I pointed my pistol at the door, just above the doorknob, reached out with my other hand, and pushed the door open.

The basement was dark except for a little bit of light leaking down the steps from the door to the first floor. I swept it with light and gun muzzle. Nothing. It was clear, at least of anything that was going to show itself. The trick to dealing with this otherworldly stuff was realizing that these things can hide while you're staring straight at them. No place is clear, even after you've checked it.

I kept checking over my shoulder as I moved to the steps, after making sure I closed the door to the vault behind me. The homunculus might have been destroyed, but I was under no illusions that it was the only threat. It was just a puppet. Whoever or whatever had been controlling it was still out there. So was Ashton, and while he may have lost control of the homunculus, he was still dangerous.

I briefly wondered if the big idol down in the vault was a representation of the controlling power behind the homunculus. I brushed the thought aside; it didn't matter, and I needed to focus on finding Ashton. The homunculus had been controlled by a power that wanted Ashton to summon whatever was near or under Powell Hill. Stopping him would stop it, at least for the moment.

The first floor was quiet. Several lights were on, but there was no sound. No rustling, no movement, nothing. A quick check of the entire house confirmed it; Ashton wasn't there. I was the only human being in the house. I paused in the living room just long enough to take a frustrated breath, then headed back down. Getting mad wasn't going to accomplish anything, and we didn't have time to spare.

Naturally, the stairs seemed to have gotten longer again. It was as if the vault itself was doing everything possible to screw with us. Which might, in fact, have been the case, if there was some pernicious intelligence at work down there.

I was cradling my battered ribs by the time I got back to the central part of the vault, where Dan and Father Ignacio were still smashing the symbols inlaid into the floor, after dousing them in holy water. As I walked over to them, I had the sudden disturbing impression that the statues around the walls had moved closer to the center. When I swept my light around, though, each idol looked like it was still up against the wall. Still, I couldn't shake the feeling that they were closing in.

"He's not here," I announced flatly. "Neither are the books or the tablet he was so interested in."

Both of them looked over at me. "Powell Hill?" Dan asked.

I nodded. "Powell Hill." I checked my watch. It was later than I had thought, but we still had a couple of hours before sunset. "Even if he doesn't know what's really going on, I suspect that whatever's pushing him is going to push harder after what we've already done down here. I've got to get up there."

"We'll come, too," Father Ignacio said. "This can wait."

We gathered up our little packages of destruction and headed back to the tunnel.

Chapter 13

Whatever determined the strange shifting of the tunnels in and out of the vault, it didn't particularly want us getting out of there and off to Powell Hill. At least, that was what I took away from the fact that it took us what felt like three times as long to get out as it did to get in. There weren't any twists or turns that hadn't been there before, nor did anything pop out at us. It just took longer to get to the shaft and the ladder.

Clambering up the ladder hurt. Every time I reached above my head, it pulled at my cracked or broken ribs, and I wanted to scream. By the time I got to Dan's Bronco, I was out of breath and almost sobbing with the pain. I scrabbled at the glove compartment, dragged out the bottle of Motrin, and downed about five, trying to at least deaden some of the pain. I leaned back in the seat as we drove away from the park, and hoped that it would kick in by the time we made it to the hill. I still needed to be ready to fight.

The drive to the parking lot at the base of Powell Hill was short. The day had gone overcast while we were down in the vault, and a blustery, cold wind was blowing by the time we parked and got out. The clouds were making it darker than it would have been, even as late as the delay in the tunnel had made us.

There were at least half a dozen cars in the parking lot, but there was no one else in view. The growing lateness of the hour, coupled with the darkness of the clouds, turned the trail leading up the hill into a darkened tunnel of gnarled, bare tree limbs. It was not inviting.

We took a moment to get ready. The wind was moaning through the tree branches and the Bronco rocked and rattled when a gust hit. Dan and I checked our rifles, refilled holy water flasks, slung cartridge belts, and mentally prepared ourselves to go up the hill. I pulled the little silver crucifix out of my shirt, kissed it, and let it hang on the outside, then crossed myself and headed on up. I wasn't moving quickly; the Motrin hadn't really kicked in yet, in spite of my hopes.

I had sort of taken the lead without thinking about it, but Dan was close behind me on my left, and Father Ignacio stepped up next to him to my right. We headed up the trail in a little wedge, ready to face whatever came.

It was strange, and I never told Dan this, but I could sense a fourth person walking along with us. I couldn't tell you how I could tell; there was no sound, and I certainly couldn't see anybody. There was just a presence, next to my right shoulder. Somehow, I knew it was the cryptic guardian angel I'd met in the dream of the stone chapel. I could see the white hair, mustache, and faint smile in my mind's eye. It was heartening, knowing he was there. I wasn't suddenly bursting with enthusiasm to run up the hill and confront Ashton and his dark partners, by any means, but his invisible presence was reassuring.

The trail hadn't changed since the last time I'd walked it. Of course, it had only been a little over a week, but it sure felt longer. It was the same rocky loam punctuated with exposed tree roots. The footing was almost as treacherous as it had been on the way down that first night, especially since we were keeping our eyes on the shadows under the trees, watching for an ambush.

We didn't encounter an ambush. We ran right into a cordon.

The entire trail wasn't hemmed in by trees. There were little open spots on the way up the hill. Particularly on one shoulder, there was a meadow at least a hundred yards across. That was where we ran into the goatheads.

There were about two dozen of them, mostly clumped near the trail. They weren't in any particular formation, and they were moving around and making little bleating noises. They seemed nervous. But when we came around the bend and stepped out into the clearing, they all turned to face us and got quiet.

Now, after getting slapped around by the homunculus in what I can only describe as an underground temple to the powers of Hell, I'll admit that I didn't find a mob of goatheads as intimidating as I might have. Truth be told, I probably should have been a little more intimidated than I was, facing that mob, but I was hurt, I'd just set an otherwise apparently indestructible demonic puppet on fire, and I was getting mad.

I kept walking, straight up the trail toward the biggest knot of them. Several more were already spreading out to our flanks, but I was too angry to care.

There wasn't any communication or coordination between them; they didn't even look at each other. They were completely focused on us. For a long moment, they stood still, while I stalked up the hill toward them, then three of them charged.

That was what I was waiting for. I whipped my rifle to my shoulder and squeezed the trigger as soon as the gold dot front sight gleamed against the right one's chest. The big longarm *boomed*; it didn't seem quite as loud as it might have with the wind hammering the hill. Flame spat, lighting up the clearing, and the goathead crashed onto its face as the big slug smashed into it.

Working the lever, I shifted aim to the center one. Another thunderous report and stabbing flame. That goathead staggered under the impact, but kept coming, so I levered another round into the chamber and shot it again. It spun halfway around and fell.

Dan's .50 Beowulf roared next to me, and the third goathead almost flipped backward, half of its skull splitting away. The rest backed off, but the trail ahead was now blocked by a solid phalanx of them.

Father Ignacio put out a hand and stopped my continued drive forward. "Slow your roll, son," he growled. "The three of us aren't going to batter our way through that."

I stopped walking, and thumbed a couple more big .45-70 rounds into the rifle's tube. I was still having to get used to the fact that I only had eight rounds available; I was used to an M4, with thirty. But keeping the rifle topped off whenever I had a chance seemed like the way to go.

"If you've got any ideas, Father," I said, "I'm listening."

"Goat-men are tough," he said, "but they're not that smart, and if you hit 'em right, you can stampede them. They'll throw themselves at you with reckless abandon until they get hit too hard, then they'll panic. Look for the biggest and the meanest. Drop him, and the rest should scatter."

No sooner had he said that, than a particularly large goathead stepped up out of the central knot. I don't know how I hadn't seen this bad boy before; he was almost a head taller than the rest, broad-shouldered and thick-limbed, with a massive pair of curling ram's horns rising from his skull. He stamped the ground and roared a challenge. The bleating tone to the roar kind of took away from the effect a little.

He threw his arms wide and stamped again, dropping his head to charge. I shot him center chest.

Dan's shot was a split second behind mine. About seven hundred grains of metal smacked into the thing about where its breastbone should be. I don't care what kind of big, bad, Otherworldly beastie you might be; that's gonna leave a mark.

It was getting too dark to see the size of the hole with any clarity, but the big sucker stopped in his tracks. He swayed, looking down at his chest, then looked up at us. His heart—if goatheads had such a thing—had to have been completely destroyed. It was just taking a little bit of time for the knowledge of his death to make its way through his thick skull.

He lifted a gnarled hand to his ravaged chest and looked down at it. The swaying was getting more pronounced, but I'd already levered another round into the chamber and was drawing a bead. He was taking too long to go down.

Then he crashed on his face in the dirt.

For a long moment, nobody moved. The goatheads stared at the big corpse on the ground, even as it began to go through the accelerated decomposition I'd seen the others do outside the church. The only sound was the rising and falling howl of the wind.

They didn't run. But they didn't charge, either. They actually seemed kind of confused as to what to do.

153

"Well, anybody got any new ideas?" I asked.

Father Ignacio took a step forward, holding up that big crucifix. The line of goatheads wavered. "I think we should push," he said.

I agreed. Thumbing yet another round into the tube, I started moving forward, up the trail, toward the line of goatheads. I kept the rifle leveled, my finger hovering near the trigger.

They still didn't break, but they kind of shuffled back as we approached. I really didn't want to get in a hand-to-hand brawl with these things, but we couldn't just sit there in a Mexican standoff as the sun went down, either.

Another step. Then another. Their line still held. We were less than ten feet away now. I wanted to stop, but I didn't dare.

The big goathead's body was almost gone now, just a pile of papery, dried tissue and crumbling bones. I was about to step over it. That was when another goathead, all of about six feet away, tried to leap forward.

I say "tried" because as soon as he jerked in my direction, his hands outstretched, I squeezed the trigger, blasting him in the midsection at point-blank range. I'm pretty sure the muzzle blast scorched his hide, or would have if the bullet hadn't immediately smashed its way through it. The creature staggered backward, got tangled up in a couple of his fellows, and fell.

What followed was a short, sharp, close-quarters fight. I shot another lunging goathead before a third tried to grab my rifle barrel. I twisted the rifle down and sideways until it was level with the creature's midsection and fired. It doubled over as the bullet ripped through it, and I tore the weapon loose and shot it in the face. Dan's .50 Beowulf was booming as he went swiftly from target to target. I shot a fourth goathead in the throat as it swung for me, and it slammed into another that was trying to charge in low. I put another bullet into that one as it tried to scramble out from under its comrade. None of them were getting close to Father Ignacio.

Then the rest were scattering, bounding into the shadows under the trees and vanishing. The bodies were already starting to crumble away.

We took a moment to gather ourselves, reload, and make sure we were ready to proceed. Then it was back to slogging up the hill.

"There's going to be worse to come," Father Ignacio said. "Goat-men are cannon fodder. If there really is some heavy-duty hoodoo going on up on top of the hill, there will be more dangerous guardians waiting before we get there."

I knew he was right, though I really didn't want to think about what could be worse than a mob of goatheads at this point. More homunculi immediately came to mind, but I pushed the image out of my thoughts. I might not have the guts to go all the way up if I thought there were more than one of those things running around.

We had about three hundred more yards and two switchbacks to go to get to the top of the hill. The woods crowded close to the trail, branches intertwining overhead to block out what little light there was left in the sky.

Nothing else attacked us, or even tried to block the trail. Glimmers of what might have been eyes glinted in the dark under the trees, branches cracked—and not with the wind. There were things out there pacing us, but they didn't try to stop us. I wasn't sure why.

We finally came to the rocky clearing where Ashton had tried previously to summon the Chthonic spirit. It appeared to have changed a little.

The rock shelf that had looked like an altar earlier was covered in candles, and I mean *covered*. The open space where the Kozheozersky Tablet was sitting was barely wide enough to accommodate it, and the rest was a mass of wax and fire. Several more large stones had been set up in a circle around it, each crowned with more candles. Ashton was standing in front of yet another, this one holding the books he'd pulled out of the vault.

There was a circle of glyphs painted on the ground in what looked like luminescent green paint. At least, I hoped it was luminescent green paint. If it wasn't, things had progressed a little bit farther than we'd hoped.

As we got closer, it became clear that they had.

There was a body at Ashton's feet, and another one at the edge of the circle. Three more of the students were on their hands and knees around it, twitching and moaning. Ashton had his

155

hands spread wide and was chanting, in a language I couldn't understand. I was momentarily glad I couldn't.

Father Ignacio stepped into the clearing, raised that crucifix again, and launched into his prayers, the sound of Latin immediately clashing with the unholy noise of Ashton's chanting and the wind. It was like battle had just been joined, but could only be heard.

In spite of the wind, there was a heavy stink around the clearing, like bile and rot. The gusting wind was making plenty of noise, but over it we could hear crying as well as screaming, demented laughter. Insane gibbering occasionally rose above the rest of the cacophony, making my ears hurt. There was no sign of who or what was making the noises, either.

The clearing was alive with shifting shapes, figures of people and monsters flickering into shape and then blinking out as fast as you could look at them. I could never get a good, solid look at any of them, but what I could see was still as vivid as any nightmare, and just as horrifying. The people were tormented, mutilated, rotting. The other...things...were worse.

As I got closer to the circle, my rifle already in my shoulder, I got a closer look at one of the students on the ground. It was Trevor. His eyes were rolled back in his head, and there was vomit on his chin and the ground under him.

I felt it then—that heavy, ominous presence that I'd sensed that first time was growing closer. I couldn't pin down where it was; I suppose it's hard to set a physical location for something that doesn't have a body to speak of. I just got the sense of something big, old, and evil getting closer. And it was powerful. That much was evident without seeing or hearing it. It was like being under a building thunderstorm.

"Ashton!" I yelled, over the noise of wind and madness. "You've got to stop this now! People are dead! Don't make it worse!"

He turned to face me. There was no sanity left in his eyes. "It's too late!" he said, his voice booming over the rest of the noise. "I've come too far! The blood has been shed. There's no going back any longer!"

He pointed a quivering finger at me. "You could have been one of the chosen, Jed! But no! You chose to crawl to the Church, to that pathetic image of a crucified God! What kind of

God lets Himself be crucified? I hail the real Powers, and they will reward me! But you...you'll be taken and they'll devour you!"

I almost didn't see it coming. I was so focused on Ashton that Dan, Father Ignacio, and the stricken students had faded out of my awareness. So had the apparitions coming and going in the dark.

So when one of the images of a rotting, mutilated corpse flickered into being right in front of my face and punched me, I was caught pretty much flat-footed.

Now, I was pretty sure that the apparitions weren't actually substantial. For something unsubstantial, though, that thing packed a hell of a wallop. It actually spun me halfway around and drove me to my knees. Fortunately I hadn't had my finger on the trigger or I might have shot Father Ignacio.

It was fast. It hit me again before I could shake off the first blow, then again and again. I'd thought the beating I'd taken from the homunculus had been relentless, but this thing was worse. I tried to fend it off with my feet, but met only smoke. I swung my rifle at it, but found the same thing.

Father Ignacio stepped in and saved my bacon again. That big crucifix of his shining like fire in the glow of the candles, he stepped forward and bellowed out a command in Latin, the syllables no less powerful for his rough, biker voice. The apparition vanished.

It took me a moment to get back up. I hurt worse than I ever had before in my life. I just wanted to lie there and not move. But the figures were swirling in and out of view in an almost solid wall between me and Ashton. I was vaguely aware, through the haze of pain and horror, of Dan standing over me, his rifle in his hands, and Father Ignacio holding that big crucifix out like a shield. The apparitions swirled around it like they didn't want to get too close.

Slowly, step-by-step, the two of them advanced in front of me. If nothing else, that was what finally prompted me to get myself up off the ground. I couldn't let Dan finish this for me. However this had started, for whatever reason, I felt responsible to finish it. I'd joined up with the Order to put right what had started thanks to my foolish curiosity. I *had* to step up.

I put my rifle butt on the ground, and levered myself up. It felt like it took forever to come to my feet. When I made it up, I felt like I could barely move. My Winchester felt like it weighed ninety pounds. I took a step forward, then another. Each took monumental effort. Every inch of my body hurt.

"Father," I croaked, "Dan, step aside."

They both looked back. After a moment, without a word, they both stepped to one side.

I advanced haltingly, painfully. My silver crucifix burned on my chest. Dan and Father Ignacio fell in on either side of me, keeping pace and helping drive the wall of apparitions back.

They dissolved like so much smoke. Just like the homunculus, they couldn't withstand the sight of that crucifix, and their very form seemed to ripple with every word of prayer that Father bellowed against the storm. We pushed through the wall and then it was just us and Ashton.

He called out a name that made my teeth hurt and my ears feel like an icepick had been driven into them. "Come forth!" he cried.

"Ashton!" I bellowed. "Last chance!" I brought my rifle to my cheek and put the gold bead on his upper chest. "End this now!"

"Come forth and take these wretched souls!" he called. A hulking shape began to take form behind him. I squeezed the trigger.

The rifle bucked in my shoulder. Flame spat through the darkness and the rifle's report slammed across the hillside. The round smashed through his sternum and he fell, his invocation dying off in a sick gurgle.

Everything went quiet. The apparitions vanished. The sickly glow of the glyphs faded. The surviving students slumped into unconsciousness.

I hobbled to Ashton. He was still alive, but fading fast. There was sheer, animal terror in his eyes as he looked up at me, shuddering as the last of his life ebbed away. Then he was gone.

"It didn't have to be this way," I told the cooling clay that had once been a man. A terribly misguided one, but still a man. "It didn't have to..."

Dan's hand descended on my shoulder. "Come on, Jed. We'll call 911 down below to come get the kids. We've still got unfinished business back at the house."

I took one more look at Ashton's body, then turned and painfully followed Dan and Father Ignacio down the hill.

Chapter 14

When we got back to the house, there were lights on in the windows. I frowned at that; I hadn't thought Ashton had left any turned on. The door was unlocked but shut. I was uneasy as I limped my way inside. "I think we'd better check the upstairs before we head down to the vault," I suggested.

"We haven't got a lot of time," Dan warned. "If we're going to be out of here before the cops come sniffing around, we've got to get this done and leave. Father Ignacio and I will head down to the vault. Check the house and come join us."

I nodded and started my room-to-room search. The two of them headed straight for the basement.

The house was as empty as I'd ever seen it. I didn't see any of the strange flickers of movement or shadows that wouldn't stay put even when nothing was moving. The house seemed quiet.

But I couldn't shake a sense of menace, a feeling that there was still something very wrong, even with Ashton gone. I realized that while Ashton was gone, we'd never determined who was guiding him.

I was about to find out.

When I entered the study, there was someone sitting there waiting for me, lounging in the overstuffed leather chair I'd sat in

160

when the Ashton had first invited me in, months before. He was dressed in an impeccable black suit, his legs crossed, with a snifter of a reddish liquor in his hand. His dark hair was perfectly combed, and his black goatee was straight and pointed.

As soon as I laid eyes on him, I felt the crucifix around my neck seem to get heavier. As perfectly human as he looked, I knew this was no man. "Who are you?" I asked. I probably should have simply backed out of the room instead.

He lifted the snifter and studied it. The liquor caught the light and seemed to glow with a bloody fire all its own. "I've gone by many names, for many, many years," he said, in a deep, languid voice. "But I will confess I've always had a soft spot for...*Mephistopheles*." My gut clenched at the name. "It does roll off the tongue, doesn't it?"

He took a sip of the liquor. "I'm here to congratulate you," he continued. "Quite impressive work you've done. You've kept quite a few young people from leaving this life for the Abyss, at least for a while. I daresay a few of them you may have scared away from Hell altogether."

He turned to look at me. His eyes were black as garnets and just as human. "Of course, the professor was the prime object of my interest. His curiosity about matters of the occult has been *so* very useful. You humans have a quaint saying, 'curiosity killed the cat.' So true." He chuckled, and the sound sent a thrill of stark terror down my spine. "The good professor's interest in old stories of occultists and alchemists got him interested in creating a homunculus. Just building one wasn't enough, though. Oh, no; he had to discover the means to animate it. That gave me the opening I needed. I used the tablet as a means to tell him how to build it, and give me control of it. After that, he would listen to anything I told him."

He swirled the liquor in its glass again and took another sip. I was frozen in my tracks. "I couldn't resist having a little fun with the homunculus while it followed you—there is little more delectable to my kind than the souls of overly-inquisitive dabblers in the hidden world. I have to say, you may have interfered in my original plan, but it all worked out in the end. Professor Ashton is now safe...with us. And you delivered him to us. You snuffed out his life before he could even think about repentance or the eternal price of his curiosity. I had originally

hoped to ensnare him by guiding him to summon my servant--"
he pronounced the same mind-searing name that Ashton had been
calling upon "--and condemn himself and his followers that way.
He would have been devoured in the very act of congress with the
Abyss. You killed him before that could happen, but the overall
effect was the same. You may as well have served him up to me
on a silver platter." He lifted his snifter in salute. "Thank you,
oh, *so* much."

My heart was thudding in my chest, the blood roaring in
my ears with a terror that went deeper than simply being in the
same room with a prince of the Abyss. Was it true? Was I
responsible for delivering the professor's soul to Hell? I hadn't
thought I'd had any other choice but to kill him, but had I simply
played into the Devil's hands?

I felt a hand on my shoulder. A glance behind me showed
me a weathered, reassuring face, framed by white hair and a
thick, white walrus mustache. The electric blue eyes were
focused on the figure in the chair.

The demon's face had stiffened slightly. "Of course, you
have nothing to fear from me, for the moment," he said. His face
seemed gaunter, more skeletal, and less human by the moment.
"My *little brother*"—he hissed the words—"is here to keep me
away from you."

With the angel at my back, I felt some of my terror ebb
away. I reached into my shirt and pulled out the silver crucifix,
letting it dangle on my chest. The demon visibly flinched at the
sight. "I think you'd better leave," I said.

He glared at me. When he spoke again, I noticed his
teeth were all sharp, like a shark's. "You have our attention now,
Mister Horn," he said. "We will be seeing you again." Then he
was gone.

My knees buckled and I collapsed to the floor. The
weight of his accusation felt like it would crush me. Had I really
damned a man?

A strong hand drew me to my feet. For the moment, the
angel seemed as physically solid as any man. He pulled me up
and held me by the shoulders, looking into my eyes. "Listen to
me, Jed," he said sternly. "The devils are liars, and that one no
less than most. You don't have the power to condemn a man; only
his own choices can do that. You did what you had to do. You

162

probably saved those four kids who survived, and who knows how many others who might have fallen victim to that spirit's influence. Trust me; it would have torn this town to pieces. Duty isn't always pretty; you should know that.

"This is why I'm allowed to talk to you like few others of my kind are," he continued. "You are running a risk being this close to the things of the Abyss. You need my help. But just like you can't control Ashton's choices, I can't make you listen. You've got to trust that I will always speak the truth, and tonight I'm telling it to you straight; you did not condemn Ashton. He did that himself. You had to stop him, and you did. That's all."

It was hard, but I nodded. No sooner had I indicated my acceptance than he was gone, just as suddenly as he'd appeared.

An hour later I was in the passenger seat of Dan's Bronco, watching as the blaze from the study began to gnaw at the rest of the house. I hadn't had to do much; there had been candles burning in the study during the conversation with the demon that called himself Mephistopheles, and I'd simply tipped one of them over onto a big enough pile of books and papers to make sure it caught. It should look like an accident. Hopefully, any occult artifacts that might lead someone else down the same road Ashton had taken would be completely destroyed.

There would be questions asked. There always are; three dead bodies, one of them dead of a gunshot wound, and a house where the gunshot victim had lived burned to the ground. But we'd been cagey with our identities; Dan had engaged very few people in town, and the students only knew my first name, aside from Ari, anyway, and he wouldn't talk. He'd already left town.

In a way, I thought, as the fire dwindled in the rear-view mirror, it was a fitting end to this chapter of my life. I'd started down the same wrong path that Ashton had. That blaze behind us was the symbol of my rejection of that way. I was on a new path. Just as dark, in a way; I would be frequenting the shadows of the world and confronting evils that that most people never dreamed existed. But now I knew that it was right, and that someone had to stand against the darkness. Why not me?

Hopefully, the old nightmares were over...

Acknowledgements

Special thanks to my wife, my Dad, and my friend Mike Kupari for giving this manuscript a good once-over. This one was a little rough to begin with, and their feedback has helped refine it immensely.

Thanks also to everyone who has read and reviewed my work; reviews help indie authors and get the word out.

Made in the USA
Monee, IL
22 December 2021

86830172R00100